Clutch

HEATHER CAMLOT

Red Deer Press

Published in Canada by Red Deer Press,
195 Allstate Parkway, Markham, ON   L3R 4T8

Published in the United States by Red Deer Press,
311 Washington Street, Brighton, MA 02135

10 9 8 7 6 5 4 3 2 1

Red Deer Press acknowledges with thanks the Canada Council for the Arts
and the Ontario Arts Council for their support of our publishing program.

Library and Archives Canada Cataloguing in Publication
Camlot, Heather, author
Clutch / Heather Camlot. -- First edition.
ISBN 978-0-88995-548-6 (paperback)
I. Title.
PS8605.A535C58 2017 jC813'.6 C2017-902211-3

Publisher Cataloging-in-Publication Data (U.S.)

Names: Camlot, Heather, author.
Title: Clutch / Heather Camlot.
Description: Markham, Ontario : Red Deer Press, 2017.
Summary: "A coming of age story set in historic and diverse Montreal,
where a young Jewish boy dreams of a brighter future just as Jackie Robinson
is making history with baseball's Montreal Royals" – Provided by publisher.

Identifiers: ISBN 978-0-88995-548-6 (paperback)
Subjects: LCSH: Jewish children – Canada -- Juvenile fiction. I Robinson, Jackie,
1919-1972. -- Juvenile fiction. I BISAC: JUVENILE FICTION / General.
Classification: LCC PZ7.C365Cl IDDC [F] – dc23

Edited for the Press by Peter Carver
Text and cover design by Tanya Montini
Printed in Canada

In memory of

My dad, Morris, and his big brother, Irving.
You started me on this journey.
I wish you could have been there at the end.

I felt a lump in my throat each time a ball was hit in his direction those first few days; I experienced a sort of emptiness in the bottom of my stomach whenever he took a swing in batting practice. I was constantly in fear of his muffing an easy roller under the stress of things. And I uttered a silent prayer of thanks as, with closed eyes, I heard the whack of Robinson's bat against the ball.

— Sportswriter Sam Lacy, *Baltimore Afro-American*, March 16, 1946

Chapter 1

AT BAT

❝ *It is no exaggeration to say that nothing that has happened in baseball in recent years is comparable to this experiment..* ❞
– Sportswriter Baz O'Meara

JUNE 1946

I think I'm going to throw up. I haven't even run two blocks and sweat is pouring down my face, I can't breathe, and I'm pretty sure the air to my brain is thinning.

But I can't slow down. I can't slow down for anything.

"Go, Joey, as fast as you can!" Ma had yelled before I bolted out the door, down the stairs of our second-floor flat, and onto De Bullion Street. She looked terrified. Her skin so pale, her eyes open real wide, and her body shaking—so much shaking. That's not the way you want to see your mother. I'm glad I got to run away. Even if it means a throbbing stitch in my ribs.

I crash into the pharmacist's door, forcing it open. I catch it on the rebound and hold onto it, doubled over, my chest heaving, trying to find the breath to speak.

"Joey!" Mr. Kis looks me over from head to toe, one eyebrow raised. "What's the matter?"

"Aspirin ... need Aspirin," I squeak, scanning the store for the familiar yellow and brown label.

"Why?" he asks, coming around with a chair. I don't need questions or a chair. Okay, maybe the chair.

"Pa's sick ... he's sweating, breathing funny ... keeps grabbing his arm, rubbing his jaw—"

"You don't need Aspirin, Joey. Go home! Now!" He grabs the telephone. I straighten up and race out. Great. Swell.

Everyone and everything I pass is one big blur. No idea what's going on around me. Don't really care. All I can focus on is getting home. Without the Aspirin. Why didn't Mr. Kis give me the Aspirin? Ma's going to kill me for not getting the Aspirin.

As I reach our flat, I hear a siren. As I go inside, I see Ma, still shaking. As I run to my parents' bedroom, I smell death.

Chapter 2

BASES EMPTY

❝ From here on there is going to be a lot of attention paid
to the Royals because Jackie Robinson
is making the great experiment. ❞
— Sportswriter Baz O'Meara

Never in my life has Pa closed our family grocery store, even for a day. Not when I was born twelve-and-a-half years ago. Not when my brother, David, was born six years later. Not for any of the Jewish holidays when Ma drags David and me to synagogue—kicking and screaming, "Why doesn't Pa have to go?"—to listen to the rabbi drone on for hours about God knows what.

We can't afford to be closed, even for a day. But a sign reading, *Closed due to death in the family*, has been hanging smack in the middle of the glass door for seven days, the Jewish period of mourning. Pa would go nuts if he knew. But seeing as he's the one who's dead, there's not much he can do about it.

I tear down the sign and yank the door wide to let in some fresh air. Instead, I'm hit with a nasty smell of horse poop. The ice cart must be nearby. I'm convinced the horse that pulls it waits for our street to drop it all. On top of that, there's a stink of garbage rotting from the heat. Great. Swell. I wedge a wooden block between the door and the frame and head to the counter to write up today's to-do list.

"Morning!" My best friend, Ben, wanders through the open door with a huge smile and half-closed eyes.

"Whatcha doing here?" I ask, surprised. Six AM is not a time recognized by Ben.

"Thought you could use the company. First day and all."

First day and all. It's not like I haven't done this a million times before. I know how to open the store, how to stock the shelves, how to charge the customers, how to bag the groceries, how to add up the receipts, how to deal with the bank.

I did it all with Pa.

I can do it all without him.

I guess it's kind of nice to have company, though. On the first day and all.

"Thanks," I say.

Ben nods, rummages through his front pocket, drops some coins on the counter, and grabs a box of Cracker Jack before settling down on his regular perch, an overturned orange soda crate. He stretches out his lanky legs that I always have to jump over because they're as long as the store aisle is wide. He unrolls the magazine stashed in his back pocket. The June issue of *Movie Life* with a real girl-next-door Rita Hayworth. Ma thinks Ben should be in the movies—the classic good looks of Frank Sinatra, she says. She would know. She tacked up the cover of Ben's March issue of *Movie Life* with a smiling Sinatra, as big as life, behind the counter.

Ben digs into his required reading and I get back to my to-do list:

- Pick up fresh loaves of bread from St. Lawrence Bakery
- Go through the credits to see who owes us money
- Get that money.

Whenever people talk about Pa, they call him a real kind man, a real *mensch*. He'd give anyone store credit. You don't have to be a millionaire businessman like Simon Bernstein to know that letting customers walk out with free groceries is a terrible money-making strategy. I'm definitely sure it's the reason we're trapped in this dump of a neighborhood.

Think it can't be that bad? There's a rumor going around that a baby's ear was a rat's dinner. Ate it off while the kid was sleeping. People call it a rumor because they don't want to believe it's true. But I've seen the red-eyed, long-toothed rats. I've heard their hissing and screeching and scurrying in the rafters of our flat above the store. They terrify me, but I play it brave for David, who's afraid to sleep because he thinks he'll be missing a body part in the morning. I tell him rats don't like smelly six-year-olds. He buys it every time, but it's getting harder and harder to get him to take a bath.

We're not going to be trapped here much longer. My bar mitzvah may not be until October, but I became a man the minute Pa dropped dead. It was living in this dump that killed him, I know it. But it's not going to get us, too.

Forget about kindness. Forget about credit. We're doing things my way now. I'm gonna get us the money and get out of here—fast. Away from the rats and the horse poop and the garbage. Away from the poor folks on De Bullion on the east side of Park Avenue, and over with the rich folks in Westmount on the west side.

Chapter 3

GROUND RULES

❝ *Today Jackie Robinson, first colored ball player
to step forth in a regularly scheduled game
in organized ranks, gets his big chance.* ❞
— Sportswriter Baz O'Meara

JULY 1946

Today's exciting midday activity for David and me is trying to get the dirt off the store's front windows. The yellow and burgundy letters on the left side say *Bernier et fils*. I have no idea who this Bernier was, but I do know he won't come off our window.

Thwack.

Wetness trickles down the back of my neck and soaks into my shirt. There's a balled-up rag by my feet. I turn to David. He's got that loopy grin on his face, that I-did-something-bad-but-I'm-too-cute-to-be-yelled-at look. You know that look? He's got it down pat. He's also got a good arm. He's practicing to be the next Jackie Robinson.

Montreal may be a hockey town but, this summer,

everyone's talking about Jackie, the first colored guy to sign a contract in modern organized baseball—and he signed it with our Royals! The *Montreal Daily Star* called it "a great experiment in justice and equality," and people from all over Canada and the States are watching. People who never even cared about baseball before. Jackie's been playing three months now, and they say he's going to change the game forever. That's a lot of pressure for one guy.

I know how he feels.

"Quit using all the water, David—we're not going to have enough." I try to sound angry but it comes out with a laugh. He's giggling like crazy, while squishing his hands through the bucket's soapy water like a pig rolling around in mud. He's as dirty and smelly as a pig, too.

It's so hot and humid this July that we're all stinking something awful. I bet the rich doctors and lawyers living on the west side of Park Avenue can smell us, and they're at least ten blocks away. It'll mean a trip to the Schubert Bath later on. There's no way I'm heating buckets of water on the stove so we can wash at home. Not that standing in line with reeking, sweaty people to get into the public bath is any better, especially when the stench mixes with the mouth-watering smell of smoked meat from Schwartz's Deli down the street.

"Joey," Ma calls from inside the store. "Mr. Friedman should be home from his newsstand, but only for a short while."

Time to deliver the groceries. And get the money Old Mr. Friedman owes us. I wipe my hands on my trousers, grab the tray of empty cups (my successful money-making idea: pour in orange soda, add popsicle sticks, freeze, sell for three cents each), and go inside. Ma's sweeping the floor, even though it's spotless. I'm not sure what she's trying to clean up. Maybe the mess Pa left us in.

I climb the stairs to our flat and drop the profit from the popsicles into my piggy bank. *Montreal Capital and Commerce Bank* is written across the front of the metal box. It has a coin slot at the top, a paper money slot on the side, and a keyhole dead center. I have to go to the bank to open it, since I have no idea where the key is. I don't even know if I ever got one. David's got the same metal piggy bank. Pa, too, but his is collecting dust somewhere. I call it the "West of Park Avenue Fund," and real soon it'll be stuffed with dollar bills, not just pennies. It'll be just enough to get us out of here.

"Clean clothes to walk down the street?" Ma asks when I come back in a blue short-sleeve shirt and navy trousers.

"Business basic #1: Look professional at all costs. It's in the book I've been reading." I wave the copy of *Get Busy, Get Rich: 10 Business Basics* that I keep at the counter for when things are slow. I've read it so much I have it memorized. It's how I came up with the idea of selling popsicles. Business basic #2: Meet a need. Hot weather, cool treat.

"I see. So as long as you're all dressed up, we don't have to worry about customers coming in."

I'm about to answer, but then I realize she's mocking me. She brushes up the invisible pile of dirt and dumps it in the garbage can behind the counter.

"Take your brother with you," she says as she pushes Old Mr. Friedman's grocery bags across the counter to me.

"Aw, Ma, it takes twice as long with him."

"Then let him sit in the wagon."

"Then where will I put the groceries?"

"He's six, Joey. He can squeeze in between," she replies.

"But I can put three customers' groceries in there and save time by delivering them all at once. Time is—"

"Time is money. Yes, you've told me." She leans against the back wall. She looks sympathetic but exhausted. "David could do with a little fresh air and a nice stroll with his big brother," she explains, with the kind of smile that would make you do anything for her. You know that smile? She's got that smile down pat.

"All right," I say. "But he's walking the whole way so I can do more than Old Mr. Friedman's order."

"As you wish, Mr. Bernstein." She smiles at her little joke. It's no joke. I will be as rich as Simon Bernstein one day. His family came to Montreal from Russia with nothing, just like Ma and Pa. But he made tons of money, making and selling cigars and cigarettes, has a mansion in Westmount, and everyone knows his name. I'm also gonna have fancy cars and fancy servants and fancy artwork hanging in my fancy Westmount house on the west side of Park Avenue. I will. You watch.

Chapter 4

PATIENT HITTER

❝ I'm not too greatly concerned over whether they succeed or fail as candidates for organized ball. What I am interested in is OUR ability to take it. ❞
– Sportswriter Sam Lacy

"Come on, David, let's go."

David runs behind the counter to grab his baseball and bat and drags it across the store and out onto De Bullion Street. It's hot and there's not one tree to offer an inch of shade. It's all bricks and concrete outside. All rats and cockroaches inside.

"I hate this street," I mutter.

We head to the butcher shop and the chicken shop just around the corner. I made a deal with them. I do their deliveries with ours, so it doesn't take any extra time, and I pocket the money they pay me for my West of Park Avenue Fund. I pack their deliveries in the wagon and head to Old Mr. Friedman's triplex. I'm sure one big gust of wind will bring the whole house down one day soon. I roll the wagon onto the patch of dirt by the sidewalk. If a flower ever tried to grow there, it would suffocate before it ever broke through the ground.

Suffocated—that's how I feel. Stuck in a Jewish ghetto where most adults speak not English, not French, but Yiddish, a language that's been dead for, I don't know … a thousand years? Honestly, living in this dump is like living in some "Old Country" *shtetl* that old people are always talking about. According to the paper, Montreal is the civil aviation capital of the world, and we're building this superfast airplane called the North Star for the air force, and even for regular people to travel. Traveling in an airplane, how amazing would that be? But folks here, in this neighborhood, they're stuck in the past, pickling their own pickles.

David runs up the rusted metal staircase, bat thudding on every step, and knocks on the door.

"*Shalom*, David! *Vos machstu*?" Old Mr. Friedman cries out, then smiles as David gives him a great big hug. It's afternoon, but Old Mr. Friedman's gray trousers and work shirt look like they've been slept in, and his white hair's standing every which way, except for what's flattened under his *yarmulke*.

"How's your mother?" he calls down to me.

Pa's been dead three weeks now, but people keep asking. They keep asking, but they don't really want to know. They ask and then they look away, to a cloud in the sky, an ant on the ground, an invisible person passing by. How's my mother? Well, if you really want to know, Mr. Friedman, she's been real busy, cleaning the flat, the store, our clothes, the dishes, and anything else she notices the smallest speck of dirt on. Things are sparkling. Things that probably didn't sparkle before. Things that were probably never meant to sparkle. As for her nights, well, she's busy then, too, Mr. Friedman. She's busy crying her eyes out when she thinks David and me are asleep. Yep, she's just dandy, Mr. Friedman.

"She's all right," I answer as I walk up the stairs. Ma would kill me in a second if I said out loud what I really wanted to say.

When I reach the top step, I stop cold. Mr. Friedman's staring at me hard, a glum look on his face. What did I do? I know I didn't say anything out loud. Wait, did I? Nah. I gulp and raise my eyebrows in an are-you-gonna-let-me-in-on-it kind of way, but he doesn't bite. He doesn't look away. No imaginary cloud, no imaginary ant, no imaginary person. Maybe he really wants to know. I don't know why. What could he possibly know about losing someone, living here alone forever? I wait, loaded down with groceries, arms getting tired, sweating from the heat.

He smiles a kind smile and chuckles just a bit. I feel like maybe he's playing me. Or reading my jumble of thoughts.

"Spitting image of your pa, Joey. More and more every day."

I know I look like Pa. I see him every day in the mirror. Every day, a dead man staring right back at me. And nothing I can do about it. What does Old Mr. Friedman expect me to say?

"Are you boys working hard?" I swear he's reading my thoughts, changing the subject like that.

"Yes, sir!" David says with a grin.

"Ah, then you should be rewarded." Old Mr. Friedman pulls out a new roll of Life Savers from his shirt pocket and unwraps one end. David's eyes get bigger, and I swear he's already drooling as he nabs the first candy. Cherry.

"How about you, *boychik*?" He looks as tired as Ma. His eyes are all puffy and his skin all droopy.

"No, thank you, Mr. Friedman," I say.

"Three months before the bar mitzvah and you think you're already too old for candy? There's plenty of time to be an adult, Joey. You need to enjoy being a child."

I can't remember ever being a child.

"I oughtta bring the food in or it'll spoil." I'm still balancing his two bags against my chest. He opens the door wide.

"*Boychik*, you read the paper? The Waldman girl was killed by an automobile just around the corner. Her brother's scooter broke, she bent over to pick up the pieces and … *Oy*. Five years old."

I nod, walk through the gloomy flat, and put the groceries

on the kitchen counter. I try desperately hard not to breathe in the foul smell of … ech … I don't even know what it is but, mixed with the heat, it's awful.

"Is everything okay?" I ask Old Mr. Friedman, thinking maybe it's a rotting rat. I really think it could be. I take a quick look around, but the curtains are closed and there's not a sliver of sunlight coming through. Not one lamp turned on.

"All's *gut*."

"Are you sure?" I wonder if he's lost his sense of smell. I think that can happen when you get old, like losing your eyesight and your height.

"I'm sure."

"Okay. Well, we'll be on our way once we're clear."

"Put it on my tab," he replies, businesslike.

"You gotta pay today, Mr. Friedman."

"*Oy*, Joey, I don't have the money right now. You know, your father—" he starts.

"My father would smile and say, 'Sure,' because he was a real kind man, a real *mensch*. I know. I'm not him. If it's a problem, I can just hold onto the groceries until you're ready." I move toward the kitchen to collect what's legally mine.

"Joseph Grosser." Old Mr. Friedman pulls the full-name threat. I stop and turn around.

"Yes, sir?" I mutter not-so-innocently. I catch David standing by the door, his eyes begging. I know he wants me to back down. I know he just wants to go home. I want to go home, too. With money in my pocket. Or groceries back in the wagon.

"Your father and I, as I was about to say before you cut me off, had a deal. I paid on the first of every month. And if you check, Master Grosser, you'll see I have always paid on time. I admire your *chutzpah*. You're a regular Bernstein. But you will leave the groceries and I will pay you on the first. Now, if you would like me to take this up with the proprietor of your business ..."

Great. Swell. Adult-speak for he's going to tell Ma.

"Fine," I spit out. "But if you're late ..." Then what? What would I do, slug him? He must be a hundred years old.

"You know I won't be."

I pull David outside and race down the stairs, my hand burning on the metal railing that's hot, but not as hot as my anger. The metal clatters in my ears with every step, but not enough to block out Old Mr. Friedman calling after me.

"You're a good boy, Joey. Your father would be proud."

Proud that I'm a pushover, like him? Great. Swell. I grab the wagon's handle and double-time it to the next stop. I'm so mad I could slug someone.

"Joey, wait up." David's little voice makes me cringe.

I glance over my shoulder to see him a good twenty feet behind. I stop and watch some kids in an alleyway playing jacks under laundry lines full of clothes, while I wait for David to catch up. The air smells like pickled herring and chopped liver. "You can't give credit, David. We need the money," I tell him straight. "You remember that."

He nods quickly and takes a big breath when he finally reaches me. I should be taking him to the park to play ball, not to people's houses begging for money.

I knock on the Druckers' door, shove a bag of groceries into Danny's arms, and stand the way I think a henchman would stand waiting for payment. Feet fixed in place. Arms crossed. Eyes narrowed.

"What's eating you?" Danny asks with a dumb look on his face. He's actually an okay guy and I feel kinda bad. He's always at the Y playing basketball or studying. Says he's going to be a doctor. With all the falls and beatings I hear he takes on the court, that's probably not a bad idea.

"Nothing," I say, standing down. "Your ma leave the money?"

"Yeah, yeah. Here." He drops a handful of coins into my hand and I count it quickly, making sure to move each coin into my other palm as I go.

"You're short." I know I'm right, but I count again anyway.

"You sure?" he asks. The question comes out so obvious that I stop counting and glare at him. So much for being an okay guy.

"Just hand it over." I try to sound threatening, but it

comes out like a whiny girl. He doesn't move, so I close in to take back groceries for the second time today. He just stares at me like maybe I've lost it. I'm definitely going to lose it.

"It's only ten cents, Joey." He says this like it will make a difference. It's my money.

"Only ten cents? Well, that's only about one loaf of bread." I grab for the loaf sitting at the top of the bag snug in Danny's left arm, but he pulls it back.

"Give me the bread or give me the money," I say angrily, planting one foot so he can't close the door on me. My right fist is tightening and even though I've never slugged anyone, it seems like the only way to get anywhere.

Danny puts down the groceries and steps right in front of me. He's almost six feet tall and only a grade higher than me in school. My breathing is heavy and my body is scorching from the inside out, but I don't back down. I don't care how big Danny is. He should be afraid. Very afraid.

I look up to stare him down. But Danny's not looking at me. He's looking over me, distracted by the *plunk* sound behind me. *Plunk*. Silence. *Plunk*. Silence. Danny reaches into his pocket and pulls out the ten cents.

"I just wanted to get a snack after basketball," he says, stepping back. I open my hand. He drops the dime into my palm and I pocket it.

"Take it from your pa, not me."

"Yeah," he mutters. "See ya around, Joey. Bye, David."

David.

David's tossing his ball in the air and catching it. *Plunk.* Silence. *Plunk.* Silence. His dark brown eyes slice right through me. His mouth and nose and forehead are all scrunched up like he's just tasted something rotten. Or seen something rotten.

"Sorry," I whisper. He catches his ball a final time and we head back to the store. Slowly.

"I'm getting us money, David. Imagine a real house on the west side, with our own rooms and a garden for Ma, and a yard for you to play ball, and neighbors who are far enough away they can't hear what we're saying though the walls."

"That's gotta be an awful lot of money, Joey. Whatcha gonna do, rob a bank?"

"Very funny. According to my book, business basic #3 is build up your business—that's what I'm doing. So far, I got the store and the deliveries. I got other ideas, too. You'll see, David. We're gonna have lots by my bar mitzvah. That's the plan. I can do it, too. Then we'll get out of this dump and never want for anything."

"I don't want for anything now." He watches my face to see if he can get away with that answer. Everybody wants something. Everybody. A medical degree. A spot in the majors.

A real life on the west side of Park Avenue.

"Nothing?" I ask suspiciously. He takes a real deep breath for such a little kid.

"I want Pa," he says without looking up. "I know I'm not supposed to talk about him and all—"

"Why aren't you supposed to talk about him?" I stop walking and face him. He stares at his bat, a thick branch of a maple tree he found on the ground in our local park, Fletcher's Field. Pa sawed and shaped it during his downtime in the store. It doesn't hit too well but it's nice to look at.

"You don't talk about him."

I open my mouth to speak but I'm not sure what to say. He's right, I don't. I don't want to talk about him. What for? He's gone. He's gone and we're here. I hate him for leaving us like this. I hate him! My eyes sting and my nose feels like it's going to drip. I sniff back hard.

"You can talk about Pa." I breathe out heavily. I mess his mop of jet-black hair and force an I'm-always-here-for-you smile. You know that smile? It's a phony smile. But it's all I've got.

"No fooling?" he asks, his eyes real big. I really don't want to talk about Pa.

"No fooling."

"I miss him."

"I know."

"Do you miss him?" he asks quietly. I feel him watching me, studying me, but I start walking again. I don't have time for this.

After a minute of only hearing his quick steps trying to keep up, David pipes up again, his voice rascally. "Do you know what else I want?" I glance over to see him smirking.

"Could've sworn a minute ago you said you didn't want for anything."

"Just one more." He pulls out a piece of folded-up *Montreal Daily Star* from his shorts pocket. I roll my eyes and smile as he unfolds the ripped-out sports page.

"You gotta read it to me, Joey! I gotta know what it says! There's a picture of Jackie Robinson and everything! I thought everyone hated him!"

"Hard to keep hating someone who works hard and wins."

"But those other people still hate him. I heard it on the radio. They don't like him 'cause he's another color."

"Yep. Doesn't help that he and the Royals are clobbering all the other teams, too."

I stop outside the store, take the paper from him and scan it. It's definitely about Jackie Robinson, but it's a long article.

"What's it say? Is it good or bad? Are those bad folks still throwing stuff at him? I gotta know, Joey!"

"I'll read it to you before bed, okay, but basically some reporter from the *Toronto Globe and Mail* is calling Jackie

Robinson a big leaguer in the near future."

"Boy, I hope someone calls me a big leaguer in the near future, Joey!"

"One day we'll go to a real ballgame, David. You'll see."

"Really, Joey? Really?" He's so keyed up, he'd bounce to the moon if I let him. I give him a squeeze and a big smile. He pops an orange candy in his mouth, his cheeks moving in and out like a fish as he sucks hard.

"Did you get that from Old Mr. Friedman?"

"Yeah."

"You shouldn't do that." I open the door to the store.

"Do what?" he asks.

"Take candy from him."

"Why?"

"Because he doesn't have enough money to feed himself, never mind feed you, too."

"But he's nice."

"You think anyone who gives you food is nice."

"That's true." He looks up at me with those smiling eyes and that loopy grin. I roll my eyes and sigh, which gives him the giggles. So much for trying to set him straight. We step into the store.

Ma is not alone.

Chapter 5

BRUSHBACK

❝*Baseball is their bread and butter
and they aren't likely to risk the displeasure
of Mr. Rickey by being openly hostile.* ❞
– Sportswriter Dink Carroll

"Can you put it on my tab, dear?" Mrs. Abelson asks, all gushy and sickly sweet. "Maxie hasn't given me this week's shopping money, and I'm afraid—"

"It's been five weeks since you last paid, Mrs. Abelson," I say, sidling up to Ma behind the counter. She's looking awfully tired, but she still gives me her say-nothing-if-you-have-nothing-good-to-say look and turns back to Mrs. Abelson. But I jump in again.

"You know, if you want free food, you can go to—"

"Joseph." Ma doesn't yell. She doesn't even get mad. She just says my name. It's in a tone that chills me to the tips of my toes and makes me want to hide in the rafters with the rats. Mrs. Abelson's eyes bounce like a ball between us.

"I understand your situation, Mrs. Abelson," Ma continues, full of respect. "But please, next week. I have to put food on my table as well. The boys, they need to grow into healthy men."

Mrs. Abelson pinches David's cheeks. "Those cheeks feel pretty round to me. But next week, Mrs. Grosser. Thank you."

"Joey will carry your groceries home for you. Won't you, dear?" she says with a smile.

I grab the groceries off the counter.

Outside, just around the corner, a bear of a man in a dark brown suit leans against the store's brick wall. A dark brown fedora shades half his face. He lowers his head to light a cigarette and sucks hard, then lets out a long wisp of smoke. He tips his hat to Mrs. Abelson, who shoots him a piercing stare.

But the man's looking at me now. His eyes are all bloodshot, like he hasn't slept in a long time. He seems familiar and unfamiliar all at once, like an actor in a movie. If I'd actually ever seen a movie.

"Joey, we must hurry." Mrs. Abelson starts walking fast, but seconds later the man steps in front of her. She stops dead.

"It's been a long time, Joey." His voice is a low growl, like gravel, but not creepy like I'd expected. It's actually kind of gentle. "Do you remember me?"

"Um … yes, sir … I think so, sir," I say, trying to keep my knees from knocking and my voice from squeaking. I remember now. He's Ben's pa, Mr. Wolfe, but I haven't seen him since the first day of Grade 1, the day Ben and I made a pact to be best friends.

"Nice of you to be carrying Mrs. Abelson's groceries, Joey. Very nice, indeed." Mr. Wolfe says. "I'd say a service like that ought to be paid for … don't you agree, Mrs. Abelson? Purchases ought to be paid for, too. Not to mention debts and loans."

"You're nothing but a crook," she says.

"A crook is someone who takes something without putting up something in exchange. Whatdja exchange for those groceries?" Mrs. Abelson doesn't answer, but she does have a huge vein popping out the side of her neck.

"That's what I thought. The kid's got enough problems, Mrs. Abelson, he doesn't need you and—"

Suddenly, Mrs. Abelson lashes out like nothing I've ever heard before, not from Mrs. Abelson, not from anyone. Her words are fast but steady, like she's been planning what she'd say if she ever got the chance, and now she's finally able to let it all out. I don't get most of what she's saying because it's all in Yiddish, but I do understand a couple of words here and there, words Pa said one time when he dropped a crate full of chocolate on his foot, words if I ever said out loud Ma would kill me.

I'm afraid to move or say anything. She slows down with a very clear *"a mise meshune oyf dir."* Don't ask me why, but I know that one. She just wished him a horrible death. I don't know why she'd wish that. Just for talking honest to her? I wonder if she wanted to wish that on me, too, when I was talking honest in the store.

She stops. I'm not sure if she's done talking or if she just needs to catch her breath. I glance at Mr. Wolfe. A lopsided smile crosses his face.

"Come on now, Mrs. Abelson, what are you teaching the kid, talking like that?"

Mrs. Abelson spins around and charges away. I stare and back away slowly, then turn and take off after her with the groceries.

When I get back to the store, Mr. Wolfe's gone. And Ma's sweeping. Again.

"That took a long time—did you help Mrs. Abelson unpack the groceries as well?"

"Huh? Oh, no." I move behind the counter to check the IOUs, which are written on nothing more than a brown paper bag.

"Joey." She puts down her broom. "Your behavior was unacceptable. You have to be polite to the customers if you want them to come back." She takes the long list away from me and slips it back under the counter.

"Why would I want them to come back if they're not

going to pay? Loyal customers are great, Ma, but to be a customer, you have to pay for what you're buying. Otherwise, you're a crook."

"Joey, that's a horrible thing to say! These are not easy times. People need kindness. Especially people like the Abelsons. When the soldiers returned from the war, they got jobs at the expense of people like Mr. Abelson. He hasn't been able to find work since. There are many people out of work and not enough jobs to go around."

"But we don't have enough to protect ourselves. If anything else happens ..."

Ma's eyes are glassy and her cheeks get pink, just enough to tell me she's thinking about Pa. She won't cry, though, not while I'm awake.

"We'll be fine," she says calmly.

"We won't be fine, Ma. That list of IOUs is getting longer and longer every day; David's shoes are five steps away from being completely useless; and it would be nice, just once, to close the store so the four of us can do something all together!"

Horror on my mother's face. She noticed my little slip.

"The three of us," I add quietly, like that'll fix it. I grab the money from my pocket and slam it on the counter. "Danny Drucker wanted to keep some of it for himself, but I wouldn't let him."

"What did you do?" Her voice is cool and steady, but the muscles in her face tighten up.

"I'm taking care of us, that's what I'm doing. Business basic #4: Protect yourself and your money." We stand, watching each other. I feel like an atomic ray-gun is firing through me, like in *Buck Rogers* or those comic books the guys at school are always talking about. But I can handle it. I'm not going to be the first to crack. I'm not. No sir.

I crack. "Ma, I just want—"

"I know, Mr. Bernstein. I know." She kisses my forehead, smiles that ready-to-take-on-the-world smile, and heads upstairs. "I'll try to stitch David's shoes."

Chapter 6

PINK HAT

❝ *His work will be watched with great interest from near and far.* **❞**
— Sportswriter Lloyd McGowan

"Do you think Dorothy Lamour knows her last name means love?" Ben asks, sitting on his overturned crate and eating a box of Cracker Jack. He's flipping through the July issue of *Movie Life.*

"I guess. She probably made up the name. Lots of actors do that," I answer, stacking cans of vegetable soup on a shelf. You'd think the cans were filled with lead, my muscles are so sore. I wonder if it's from *schlepping* the wagon to Mount Royal and Fletcher's Field. With the hot weather, David and me, we've been selling ice-cold drinks to the people playing and picnicking on the mountain and in the park. Business basic #5: Expand your reach. It's been a real money-maker. But the wagon's pretty heavy with all the glass bottles.

"Aha, you've been dipping into my fan magazines! There's no way they talk about Hollywood in the business section of the paper." Ben slaps his knee in triumph. I roll my eyes. He knows I couldn't care less about that kind of stuff. "So, you wanna come see the new *Road* movie with Dorothy Lamour?"

I shake my head while lining up cereal boxes. He moves behind the counter and fills up the glass candy jars.

"Come on, you won't get in any trouble—I promise."

I shake my head again. It's illegal to go to the movie theater if you're under sixteen. There was a fire in some theater twenty years ago that killed almost eighty kids. Ben's so in love with the movies he goes anyway. I don't know how he gets in. I don't ask. And I don't go. I have no interest in breaking the law. Even a law as dumb as keeping us out of the movies.

"I have my bar mitzvah lesson this afternoon," I say, grateful for an excuse.

"Oh, right. Gosh, that was such a bore. Glad mine's over with. You gonna see that girl ... what's her name, Shelly?"

"Yeah, I suppose."

"Guess I'll just have to find a girl to spend my afternoon with, too," he says, lifting his eyebrows up and down twice.

"We don't spend the afternoon together."

"Sure, not in front of the rabbi."

"Not in front of anyone!"

"Huh. Too bad. Anyway, I gotta run if I'm gonna make the movie. Have fun at your lesson. Hey, does your girlfriend look anything like Dorothy Lamour?" Ben winks and heads out.

"Shelly's not my girlfriend!" I call, but the door shuts before I finish.

A few minutes later, David charges in, trips on his laces, and falls to the floor, along with a handful of change from the popsicles he'd been selling. He lifts himself up on all fours and frantically picks up the money, constantly checking the door. The way he's scurrying makes me think of the cockroach I saw in Old Mr. Friedman's kitchen last week. When he's done, he jumps to his feet, runs behind the counter, spills the change into the till, and ducks.

"What's with you?" I ask, leaning over the counter.

"He's coming!" he squeaks, squishing himself into the corner between the counter and wall and shushing me with a finger to his lips. He shuts his eyes tight.

"Who?" The door opens and I turn to see a big round belly jut into the store, then the tip of a dark brown fedora. Mr. Wolfe. I lean back against the counter.

"Oh, hello, sir," I say. "You just missed Ben."

The giant smiles at me but his eyes dart around. They're still red, too, like those of the rat I chased out of our bedroom last night.

"Is that so?" His tone makes it sound like he missed Ben on purpose. "I hope you're not still thinking about the little spat with Mrs. Abelson the other day. Didn't mean to upset her, but she's a spirited one."

"No, sir," I lie. Actually, I haven't been able to stop thinking about Mr. Wolfe. That was the first time he's ever been around here. The first time I've ever spoken to him. Ben's been here after school almost every single day since Grade 1, but I've never been to his house. Ever. I can't even tell you what street he's on.

"You know, Benny was real upset about your father. Benny liked him a lot. I offer you my condolences."

I nod but don't look away. I can't seem to look away.

"Your father was real good to him. Real, real good to him." He says the last part slowly, every word sounding important and sincere. He leans over the counter, grabs a pack of cigarettes, and tosses down a whole dollar. "Keep the change."

That's a lot of change, way more than the cigarettes even cost. I want to pocket the extra money for my West of Park Avenue Fund, but I don't move. He lights up a cigarette and inhales for what must be ten seconds.

"How's business going?" he asks, blowing out a chimney's worth of smoke.

I wave away the smoke swirling around my head, my eyes tearing up. Mr. Wolfe wanders around the store, picking up and putting down a loaf of bread here, a jar of mustard there.

"Okay, sir," I lie again.

"Bet you got lots of people who don't wanna pay. Your father was a kind man, a real *mensch*, but not such a businessman as yourself." My stomach knots at the mention of my pa. Mr. Wolfe returns from his tour and punches me in the arm, throwing me off balance. I think it was supposed to be a friendly tap, but it hurts so much I let out a whimper.

"It's an unfortunate situation he's left you in."

"Yes, sir."

"But I'm gonna help you, Joey."

Great. Swell. Just what I need, help from a man who's been back and forth to prison for running a real rough gambling den. Gambling's also illegal in Montreal, but it's also the biggest game in town—bigger than hockey and baseball. Ben may keep what goes on at home secret, but I read the paper. I know what's going on. Everyone at school knows, too. What the kids at school probably don't know is that Mr. Wolfe could pummel any one of us into the ground with one of his bear-like paws, but when he speaks, his voice is a kind whisper.

"Thank you, sir." I try to sound sincere. Better to play it safe. I don't know if turning him down'll make him mad, and I don't really want to find out. He puts one of his paws on my shoulder. It's so heavy, I feel like I'm being pushed into the ground.

HEATHER CAMLOT

"I had a hunch you and me were the same. I can see the drive in your eyes."

I try to see my eyes from the inside. I must look like an idiot, because when I focus back on Mr. Wolfe, he's looking at me funny. When he's finished considering whether I'm as dumb as I act, he continues.

"We're business people, you and me. We know we gotta seize opportunities, make our own way. No one's gonna hand us a bag of money for free. No one's gonna get us out of this godforsaken ghetto but us. Am I right?" He's got my full attention now and he knows it. He stretches out his arm, pulls up his jacket sleeve to reveal a gold wristwatch, and checks the time. Now he's got my double attention.

"I'm gonna get to the point, kid, because I have another appointment. I've got a new business I'm working on and I need someone who's willing to roll up his shirtsleeves and take some risks. Someone who knows what he wants and will do whatever it takes to get there. Is that you?"

"Yes, sir. But what about Ben?"

"Benny's a dreamer, Joey. I need a doer."

"What's the business?"

"I can't reveal those details yet, but I'll let you know when the time's right. You understand?" He says these last two words like my life depends on understanding, but he's got a real big smile on his face that makes me smile, too. I nod real quick. "Good. I'll see to it myself you're paid well. Real well."

He leans over the counter and takes a good long look at David. "So long, kid." David's been so quiet, I forgot he was even here. But he still doesn't say anything. "Didn't your mother teach you it's impolite not to speak when spoken to?" David doesn't bite.

"Too bad you're not older, kid," he says with a quiet laugh. "I got lots of work in the gambling business for people who don't talk." He flips David a candy, fixes his hat so the brim sits low, and heads for the door.

"We're going to be good friends, Joey, very good friends. Just like Benny and your pop." He yanks open the door like maybe he thinks he's locked in.

"Oh." He looks at me one more time with those bloodshot eyes. "I'm gonna be the one to tell Benny the good news, all right?"

I scrunch my forehead and nose, not sure why he feels the need to tell me this, then nod. It's been a strange conversation. Was it even a conversation?

"Stay outta trouble."

As the door swings shut, I look over at my little brother and notice he hasn't popped the candy in his mouth.

"Guess he's a nice guy if he's giving you candy."

He stands and chucks the candy into a dish by the cash register.

"I don't take candy from strangers."

"He's not a stranger, he's Ben's pa."

"No, he's not. Ben doesn't have a pa. He told me so hisself."

"What are you talking about?"

"At Pa's funeral, Ben said all boys should have a father, and he wished he had one he could share with me." David slides down to the floor and tosses his baseball against the wall of his not-so-secret hiding spot.

I'm not sure what that's supposed to mean. Mr. Wolfe is definitely Ben's pa.

"Why'd you run in here and hide when you saw him coming?"

"He kicked a little cat that was in his way. I didn't wanna be in his way, too."

Chapter 7

CHARGING THE MOUND

❝ *It so happens that Robinson is the Pittsburgh Courier's
prize candidate for the major leagues and our interest
in his future is extremely high.* **❞**
— Sportswriter Wendell Smith

AUGUST 1946

"Ma, stop fussing," I say as she tries to make a decent part in my hair and flatten the flyaways with some hair tonic.

"It's a social, Joey. I don't know how you and Ben received invitations, but it's a great honor and you need to look your best." She grabs hold of the bottom of my dress shirt and the waist of my suit pants.

"I'm not a kid. I can comb my hair and tuck in my shirt. And you know I always try to look my best—"

"In case you should run into Mr. Bernstein himself and he hands you a one-hundred-dollar-a-week job for not looking like a *shlump*." She smiles at her little joke.

At least *I'm* trying. Whenever she's not in the store, she's got this God-awful robe on. The sleeves are completely frayed, a pocket's fallen off, and it's so washed out it looks like rotting skin. I don't say it out loud, though. Pa gave her that robe.

"Ma, stop!" There comes a time when a mother shouldn't be poking and prodding in certain areas, even if she has "seen it all before." She drops her hands to her sides and gazes at my reflection in the bathroom mirror. The little laugh lines go sad around her eyes but she doesn't say a word. Instead, she pats me on the cheek and leaves the bathroom, which isn't meant for two people, anyway, unless you like standing right up between the toilet and the sink, and with David's aim, trust me, you don't want to be right up against anything in here.

I look at myself in the mirror. It gives me a knot in my stomach. Nah, more like a punch in the gut. I hate seeing my reflection. Pa's reflection. Dirty brown hair. Long, narrow face. Hazel eyes. Thin build. No matter what I do or how hard I try, I always look back at his hair, his face, his eyes, his build.

Him.

"I'm going to do what you couldn't!" I hiss at the man staring back. "I'm going to get us to the west side of Park Avenue and get a better life!"

I pound my fists on the yellowed sink. As my eyes narrow and my mouth tightens, his face quickly disappears. I splash ice-cold water on my face to cool down. I have permanent dark circles under my eyes and these rough, dry patches on my cheeks from I don't know what. Ma thinks I should see the doctor, but I'm not wasting my time on someone telling me to get more sleep and drink more water.

"Ma, do we have cream or something?" I call out. I know, it sounds girly, but those dry spots are kinda itchy.

"In the linen closet, third shelf," she says. I take one giant step across the lifting linoleum floor and come face to face with the linen closet.

The closet is crammed with stuff. I push my way through a whole lot of Aspirin (Ma obviously doesn't want to be without ever again) and slabs of soap, and come to a pottery bottle in the back left corner. I recognize the buoy shape immediately. The bottle is heavier than it looks. I yank off the top—*pop!*— and take a whiff.

"Pa." The word comes right out of my mouth as I breathe in the familiar mix of orange, cinnamon, and vanilla. Why does Ma still have his cologne, with the "Ship Friendship" on the front and the red lettering of "Old" and "Spice" on either side of—

"Did you find it, Joey? Ben's waiting for you."

I push around the rest of the boxes and bottles, find the cream, slap some on my face, and shove everything back in. I take one more whiff of the cologne—which makes me shiver— put the top back on, and drop the bottle where I found it.

HEATHER CAMLOT

"Yeah, coming." I take a last look in the mirror, shove my shirt in my pants, and rush out of the bathroom, grabbing my suit jacket along the way. I don't even want to go to this stupid social. I should be in the store, working late and planning out the details of my side businesses. But Ben was talking about it while Ma was around and then she was absolutely set on me going. I think he planned on it rolling that way. Great. Swell.

"So handsome." Ma takes one last try at taming my hair. "Oh, we should have polished your shoes."

"Ma," I say, rolling my eyes. David's lying on his belly in front of the radio, waiting for the second game of the double header to start, and lining up the cereal-box baseball diamond and cut-out players we made after I got so irritated with him asking me a hundred times who was on which base because he couldn't keep track. Yeah, yeah, sounds like the *Who's On First* Abbott and Costello routine. It's not so funny when you're the straight man, let me tell you.

"Joey, tell Ben how they didn't play Jackie yesterday and they lost. Of course they lost!" David rants, his little fists punching the floor.

"You just told him."

"Yeah, but he doesn't understand. If he did, he'd be angry, not happy. Look at him."

I look at Ben sitting on the chesterfield. The cushion he's

on sags low, forcing Ben's knees up to his chest. He's got a hand over his mouth and his eyes are half-closed. I don't know how long this conversation's been going on, but definitely long enough that David's got Ben about to bust a gut laughing. He's desperately trying not to, but he's not doing too good a job.

David sits up and faces Ben. "If you wanna win, you gotta play the game right, and you gotta play it with your best players, Ben. It's so obvious!" David lets out a long sigh, rolls his big eyes, and throws his arms up in defeat. Forget about being the next Jackie Robinson. The kid should be the next Royals manager.

Ben takes a deep breath and gets up from the chesterfield. "I get it, David. Really. I do."

David rolls his eyes again and turns back to the radio.

"You clean up good—you look like a real *mensch*," Ben says, patting me on the back. The words echo in my brain and whirl together with the smell of Old Spice. I say nothing. Ben looks like a million bucks in his blue-gray double-breasted suit and bright-white dress shirt. Looks like they cost a million bucks, too. Between his clothes and his pa's gold watch, it seems like they have an awful lot of money. But if they did, they wouldn't live in this neighborhood. So where's the stuff coming from? I can't stop thinking about Mr. Wolfe and his promise to pay me well if I help him out. One leap closer to the west side.

HEATHER CAMLOT

"You ready?" Ben asks, heading for the door.

"Yeah, yeah. Hey, you think Dorothy Lamour will be showing up at the social?"

"I guess she could—it is in Westmount!"

Yeah, he said Westmount. The generous super-rich folks on the west side throwing the poor kids on the east side a bone. I doubt it has any meat on it, though.

Chapter 8

FREEZE THE HITTER

❝Local sports fans didn't seem to appreciate how monumental and revolutionary a move Brooklyn and Montreal ball clubs had made. ❞
— Sportswriter Dink Carroll

"Hey, how *did* you get invitations, anyway? I thought you had to be going into Grade 11." With no bus in sight, Ben keeps walking west along Pine and I try to keep up. He smiles slyly. "Oh, what does that mean?" I ask nervously. I should have questioned him before I got roped into going.

"Don't worry. If anything happens, I promise to take the heat and let you walk away scot-free."

"Like father, like son, eh?" I laugh. Ben stops dead in the middle of the street. Two streets, actually. Two busy streets. One fatal intersection.

"Ben, we're going to get killed!" My suit's starting to feel wet from sweat. It's getting awfully itchy, too. But that bothers me less than our impending deaths. He wheels around and looks at me with real menacing eyes.

"Why would you say that?" His voice is shaky and he glares at me, through me, his fists balling.

"Say what?" My eyes dart back and forth at all four directions of traffic, as cars honk and swerve around us, drivers and passengers yelling, a horse neighing in the distance.

Bang, bang, bang, bang, bang! I jump a mile in the air at what sounds like gunshots. My blood races and I'm really sweating now. I look around. A streetcar is passing. Some kid must have put caps on the tracks again.

"Like father, like son?" he whispers, like he doesn't want to hear the words again. "I'm nothing like my father!" he shouts.

"I ... I know. He said the same thing," I say desperately.

"You're talking to my father?"

"Ben, can we finish this on the other side of the street?"

He looks me over with icy eyes and moves quickly to the sidewalk. I run behind him to safety.

"Stay away from my father."

"How can I? He comes by to visit."

"What?" He stops dead again and those terrible eyes flash my way. I've never seen those eyes before. Not on Ben.

"He just comes by the store. Well, usually outside the store. He's been awful nice, asking about business and tactics and progress, and all that. He's even offered some tips on getting all the credits paid and how to make more money. He's been real ..."

I want to say fatherly but I doubt that'll go over well. Thinking about the right word, I remember David going nuts over how the sportswriters were starting to give Jackie Robinson a bit of respect: *They're all changing their minds about Jackie! They didn't like him one bit, but now they're figuring what we knew all along!* Nobody likes Mr. Wolfe, but maybe it's time to change our minds about him, too, like that whole "don't judge a book by its cover" thing teachers always go on about. I'm sure everyone who works in the gambling business must look all bloodshot and beat and smell like cigarettes and liquor. How could they not? Point is, Mr. Wolfe's been a real swell guy, trying to help. That's the word. "Helpful."

"Oh, God." Ben closes his eyes and takes a deep breath. When he opens them, he doesn't look mad anymore, but he does look worried.

"I thought you knew. He said he was going to tell you."

"Gee, it must have slipped his mind." Ben says this all sarcastic and sour. I don't get why Mr. Wolfe is keeping it a secret.

Or why Ben keeps his father a secret. "Why'd you tell David your pa wasn't worth sharing? He thinks you mean your pa is dead."

"If only," he mutters.

"What?" I must've misheard. Ben couldn't actually want someone dead. "You always hung around my pa, so why can't I hang around yours?"

Ben laughs like he's just heard the funniest joke ever, like I'm Abbott and Costello performing *Who's On First*, like I'm David ranting about baseball.

"Because you're not allowed to! That was the deal."

"What deal?"

"The deal your pa and my ma made so that we could be friends."

"What are you talking about?"

"I never had any friends before you, Joey. Parents would find out who my pa was and they'd make up excuses why their kids couldn't play with me. But your pa, he ..." Ben takes another deep breath, "... he agreed to give it a shot as long as my pa never came anywhere near you or David. But he seems to think with your pa gone, that rule's gone, too."

"I think I can judge for myself."

"Obviously you can't judge for yourself!" Ben shouts.

"Wait a minute!"

"What's your ma said about his visits, eh?"

"She ... well, she hasn't actually seen him," I say, feeling real dumb.

"Nah, 'cause he knows if she saw him, she'd hit the roof!

Your pa knew what he was doing when he made that deal and I owe him big, so I'm going to make this real easy for you." Ben's voice gets scary quiet. "Me. Or him."

"What?" My heart pounds behind my Adam's apple and tiny daggers twist in my stomach.

"You don't know my pa like I do, Joey. And you don't want to. Me. Or. Him."

I think I'm in shock. I must be. I can't speak. I can't open my mouth. I can only stare at Ben in disbelief. He's waiting. And waiting.

The bus arrives. He hops on. Without me.

Chapter 9

FORCE PLAY

❝ Never has a sports selection been more brilliantly vindicated. ❞
– Sportswriter Baz O'Meara

We've never fought before. We've never argued. I don't think we've ever even had a difference of opinion, unless you include going to the movies, and even then, that's hardly anything. He goes, I stay. He goes …

He's gone. Off to that dumb party that I never wanted to go to. He actually left without me. He stood here, sizing me up with that stare, giving me goosebumps in this boiling heat. In this boiling suit. He didn't even let me answer his dumb ultimatum. Him or his pa. Of course I'd pick him. What does he take me for, an idiot?

Maybe I am an idiot. How did I not know about this deal between Pa and Mrs. Wolfe? Why would Pa even do that? Did he think I can't take care of myself? If he was so worried about me, why'd he get sick and die? Leave.

"WHY DOES EVERYONE THINK THEY CAN JUST LEAVE?" I shout so loud my throat feels raw. I know people are staring at me, probably wondering what asylum I've just escaped from. If they're speaking, I can't hear them. Sounds are all muffled like I'm under water. The throbbing of my chest is clear, though. It's making my brain pound, like my skull's not big enough.

All of a sudden, I'm sprinting. Sprinting like Jackie Robinson as he rounds third for home. Sprinting like a kid who's about to lose his father if he doesn't get Aspirin. I catch up to the bus. I can see Ben in the window and he can see me. I know he can see me because he does that wide-eyed thing any normal person would do when watching an insane person run after a bus. It slows to a halt at the next stop. Ben is standing by the driver.

"Are you crazy?" he asks, reaching out a hand to help me on.

"Don't. Ever. Do that. Again," I say as I pull off my jacket, loosen my tie, and run my fingers through my hair to try and tame it. Like that's possible.

He pats my shoulder as we sit for the ride along Pine and Sherbrooke to a streetcar that will take us up Côte-des-Neiges Road, up to the party in Westmount. We don't speak. I don't really know what to say, anyway. Running after him like Jackie Robinson charging for home. Racing after a bus because I refuse to lose him and Pa in one summer. Maybe that's enough.

But it's not enough. I need to know. What else is he keeping from me?

Chapter 10

ONE-GAME WONDER

66 *Everyone wants to see him after reading so much about him. Right now he is something to see too. There doesn't seem to be anything he can't do.* **99**
— Sportswriter Dink Carroll

"You ready? Follow me!" Ben is all goofy as he races off the streetcar, runs along one street, then another, all uphill for what feels like forever, until we're at the very top. Then he turns into a driveway that's got to be two blocks long.

In front of us is the biggest house I've ever seen. I don't think I can even call it a house. Mansion? Castle? *Château* makes it sound even more impressive. It's got seven chimneys and an actual turret, so they can watch out for other rich folks who want to attack, I guess. I don't know how much they'd see from it, though, since the place is in its own little forest, with lots of trees and grass and hedges. That's what my street needs. Trees and grass and hedges.

"Like it? I picked it out just for you," Ben says with a smirk.

"Very funny," I mutter.

"Come on, Mr. Bernstein, let me show you your new home!" Ben dashes along the drive. Then he cups one hand under his chin, rubs one finger along his cheek, and squints like he's working real hard to figure something out. "I wonder if Mr. Bernstein's actually inside."

"Wait, what? This is really ..."

"Yep. One of the Bernsteins. Father, son ... I don't really know which one. Does it matter?"

With the possibility of meeting any Mr. Bernstein, my legs go heavy as I climb each stone step. My chest heaves like I'm pulling our wagon full of glass bottles straight up the side of Mount Royal. I check my progress. I've gone up all of two. Ben sits on the back of a stone lion as tall as David and watches me with that great big smile encouraging me on. When I finally make it to the landing, he slaps me on the back.

"Fine form, young man. Well done, I say." I don't know what movie he's pretending to be in, but I imagine he sounds like some wealthy British landowner. He slides off the lion, pats it on the head, and rings the doorbell. A man in a black suit opens the door. My knees shake. I think I'm going to pass out. I really do.

"He's the butler, Joey," Ben whispers. "Honestly, if you plan on living in Westmount one day, you ought to learn what's involved." He grunts and I roll my eyes. At least, I mean to roll my eyes. They may be fixed in place. Along with my feet.

"Invitations, please," the butler says dryly, like he wishes he had better things to do than play bouncer to a high school party.

"Good evening, sir. Our friends were to arrive before us with our invitations. If we could just find them ..." Ben begins in that same landowner tone that suggests he's spoken to super-rich folks before. Or at least to their butlers.

"No invitation, no entry." The butler starts closing the door but Ben sticks a well-polished black oxford in the way. "If you'd be so kind as to find Adele Abelson, sir."

"Adele Abelson?" I look at Ben for some sort of answer as to how she's the friend with the invitations, considering I've met her maybe once in my life, but he stays focused.

The butler searches Ben's face and I guess he decides he's okay, because he gives a very quick nod. He closes the door and I hear a grinding, then a click. A second later, a clunk. Two locks. Great. Swell. Making sure we can't break in or anything. Because that's what rich folks think poor kids do.

"Did you see? It's like *The Magnificent Ambersons* in there!" Ben gushes. I'm guessing that's a movie. I did catch the massive staircase and a fireplace for one of those chimneys. And the chandelier drooping with what must be hundreds of crystals, hanging from a ceiling so high I couldn't even see it. And the marble floor was so shiny—I bet David wouldn't give one thought to scratching and muddying it to death by dragging his bat from Fletcher's Field.

The door unlocks. Twice. "Miss Abelson was unable to attend due to a work commitment. No invitation, no entry. Good evening." The butler shuts the door. And re-locks.

I pat Ben on the back and turn from the door. "I didn't want to go to the social, anyway."

"Yeah, I know. But it would have been a gas if you got the chance to meet Mr. Bernstein."

"Fortunately for you, then, I'm right here." I spin around and come face to face with a man about the same age as Pa, wearing a real nice suit, dark tie, black-rimmed eyeglasses, and a curious smile. "Did you really have invitations?"

"I ... I ..." I can't speak.

"Good job! Never answer incriminating questions without an attorney present, boys. Gets you into trouble. My butler is a stickler. Sometimes he doesn't let *me* into the house." Simon Bernstein is talking to me. Simon Bernstein. One of the richest men in Canada. My chest pounds, like Jackie Robinson's must have just before stepping up to bat for his Minor League debut, just before smashing the ban against colored players right out of the ballpark.

"What are your names?" Mr. Bernstein asks.

"I'm Ben Wolfe, and this is my friend, Joseph Grosser. He's a big fan of yours and a businessman like yourself."

"I'm going to live here someday," I blurt out. Ben's eyes roll back in embarrassment but Mr. Bernstein keeps smiling.

"Well, let me know when you're ready to buy. Be warned, this place is a beast to keep up."

I nod slowly. That's right, Joey: up and down. Up and down.

"I'd better go in. If my butler allows it, of course. I don't have any identification on me."

"Could you let us into the party?" Ben asks, like Mr. Bernstein is just some regular guy, and not ... you know ... Mr. Bernstein.

He lets out a great big laugh. "Rules are rules, I'm afraid, and sometimes they need to be followed. You'll have your turn when you're of age—and when you really have invitations. Until then, it was a pleasure to meet you, Ben Wolfe." He shakes Ben's hand. "And you, Joseph Grosser." He shakes my hand.

"Uh-huh," I reply. Dumb. Dumb. Dumb.

Mr. Bernstein laughs and starts for the house.

"Sir!" I call out. Mr. Bernstein turns from the door with a surprised look. At least, I hope that's surprise and not annoyance. "What ... what's the secret to your success?"

"Interesting." A grin creeps onto his face as he thinks about his answer. "Make money any way you can, invest it in something worthwhile, keep searching for better and bigger opportunities, and always help others." I nod, burning his advice into my brain. Mr. Bernstein has so much money, he gives tons of it away for schools and hospitals and community centers. "And, of course, look professional at all costs." Ha! I knew it! That's the way to play ball, Joey.

"Do you ever give credit?"

"Only where credit is due. And I can say with certainty that you will be a credit to whatever you pursue, Joseph Grosser. You remind me a bit of myself. I was not born into this." He waves his arms to point out the mansion and property. "My family came to Montreal with very little. But I was curious. And curiosity usually makes one driven, creative, and ready to tackle challenges. I wouldn't be surprised to hear your name again in the future—other than when you buy the house, of course."

"Thank you, sir."

He nods and goes inside. I force my brain to send a message to my feet that it's time to move along the driveway. It works, though awfully slowly.

I imagine Mr. Bernstein repeating my name to all his business colleagues. "He'll be big in the business world, I tell you. Remember that name—Joseph Grosser. Firm handshake. What else do we need to know?" The white-haired, white-bearded men all nod their heads at the same time, trying to stamp my name in their minds.

I slap my hand on Ben's shoulder and walk with him to the road. "That was the best social I've never been to."

Chapter 11

HIT THE DECK

He's *not only a good ball player, but he conducts himself properly and keeps his head.* **99**
— Clay Hopper, Montreal Royals manager

It's almost ten-thirty and dark out by the time we walk the long road over Mount Royal to get us home. We could've taken the streetcar and bus, but Ben said he was in the mood for a walk and had never tried it before. Here's why he's never tried it: First, it's got to be three miles. Second, on one side of the road, there's this enormous cemetery. Thousands of dead people. Making my skin crawl. Third, the other side of the road is all pitch-black deserted park, which turns into these giant rock faces that feel like they're closing in on me. This walk over the mountain is no walk in the park.

To top it all off, my shoes are killing my feet and my suit is making me sweat. I just want to get home.

But Ben's got a different idea. As we come to the bottom

of the mountain road, he veers off into Outremont. Being a neighborhood just west of Park Avenue, Outremont is full of rich people and big houses and nice yards. Just not as rich or as big or as nice as Westmount.

"What are you doing?" I ask impatiently, staying on the road that leads home.

"Looking for something." Ben flashes his movie-star smile. I run, which is more like a limp, to catch up to him. He rushes up a grassy slope to a huge square house with a porch that wraps around at least two sides. Then he stands there, considering something, I have no idea what. Then he moves on to an even bigger house next door and stands there again, just staring.

"Who knew rich people had such poor taste?" he says to no one in particular. He tears back down the slope, runs across the deserted road, darts over some weird island, then crosses the street on the other side to a red-brick three-storey house. I plod after him.

"Perfect." Ben walks across the lawn of a fourth house, which somehow seems a little less intimidating than the last three, even with its turreted left side, red roof, and mix of brick and stone. The garden is so breathtaking, Ma would cry her eyes out, if she had any tears left to cry. How do you make a garden like that?

"Now what are you doing?" I whisper as loudly as possible. I want to scream it, but I'm afraid someone will hear.

"Just getting some of these flowers," he calls back loudly. He pulls out a jackknife from his back pocket and slices through the stems of a handful of lilies. I think that's what they're called, anyway.

"Someone just turned on a light," I say nervously, while watching a shadowy figure move across the closed curtains. Ben puts the flowers on the ground, folds his knife, and puts it back in his pocket. I move across to the island, hoping there's enough darkness to stay invisible.

"Can we get out of here, please?"

Ben carefully scoops up the lilies and wanders back to the sidewalk. As he walks across the street to meet me, another light goes on—just inside the front door. We hightail it back to Mount Royal Avenue, cross it, and relax once we're in the park.

Then I hear an unpleasant sound. The growl is low but clear. Ben hears it, too, and we both turn back to face the road—and a chocolate brown pit bull, still on the opposite side. Quickly, the growl turns into a bark, loud and fierce.

"That dog doesn't seem happy with us," I sputter.

"Nope."

"You think it'll make it across the street?" I ask, watching the pit bull dart from side to side, trying to keep us in view between passing cars.

"Looks like it wants to. Cars are keeping it there, though." Ben goes silent, but I'm too afraid to take my eyes off the dog to see what he's doing.

"There's a streetcar coming," he finally says. A plan. A plan is good. "When it blocks the dog, run." I'm not sure how good that plan is. I gulp. Ben gulps. The streetcar is almost here ...

"Run!" Ben screams.

"AHHHHHHHH!" I take off as fast as my aching, burning feet can go. Left foot, right foot, left foot, right foot ... that's it, Joey, left foot, right foot. I can't hear the dog behind me, but then I can't hear much of anything except the pounding in my brain and the pounding in my heart. I think I'm going to have a heart attack. I really do.

"This way!" Ben yells from the angel statue in the middle of the park. I run up the sloped grass, scramble up the slanted granite, and breathe heavily as I stand on the first ledge of the statue by some bronze figure reading a book.

"Keep going," Ben calls down from his lofty perch. How in the world did he climb the statue so quickly? So easily? Has he done this before?

"Isn't this high enough?" I beg. The monument's got to be a hundred feet high.

"Maybe." He smiles. I'm starting to hate that smile. I grope my way over the head and shoulders of the bronze girl reading and the woman sitting next to her, holding the Civil Code in her arm. The code I'll be tried with for damaging public property—and for aiding and abetting Ben's flower-stealing scheme. At least, I think that's the *Civil Code*. It's not like I ever needed to know. I never had any intention of breaking the law. My pa didn't raise me that way. I'm not even going to ask how Mr. Wolfe raised Ben. And now my life's at stake. Is that a valid defence in a courtroom?

I reach the second level and Ben, who is standing between some soldier carrying a flag and the guy the statue was built for. No idea who he is. Or why he has a statue. Or why he's got the most complicated statue in the world with so many figures on it. I can't think straight. Or breathe properly. Or stand. I drop onto the ledge, panting, and lean against the column topped by a winged angel. Yeah, another figure.

The pit bull skids to a halt and jumps but can't reach high enough. I whip my legs up against my chest anyway. He starts clawing at the base of the statue, like he plans on climbing it. Or maybe reducing it to dust.

"How long do you think we were running?" I say, still gasping for breath.

"A minute and a bit," Ben replies, not winded in the least.

"That's it? That can't be it!"

"That's it. I'm sure you would have made it sooner if you hadn't run after the bus before the party."

"Very funny," I say. Ben sits next to me and watches the jumping dog with amusement.

"He's actually kinda cute," Ben says. The dark brown fur, severe scowl, and sharp teeth remind me of Ben's father. But I'm not about to tell Ben that. I close my eyes and concentrate on slowing my breathing.

"Petey! Where are you?" At a woman's call from somewhere in the park, the beast of a dog stops growling and pawing.

"Petey! I mean it!" The voice gets closer but the woman is still hidden by the trees. With one last bark, the dog runs toward the voice and out of sight.

"Petey. That's funny!" Ben exclaims. "That's the name of the pit bull in *Our Gang*!"

"What's *Our Gang*?"

"The movie shorts? Alfalfa? Buckwheat? Bunch of poor kids and their crazy adventures?" I shake my head at everything he's saying, but it sounds awfully realistic. "You really have to come to the movies at least once."

We wait a few minutes, then climb down and start again for the east side of Park Avenue, for home. I'm glad I never bothered polishing my shoes.

"They're pretty, no? Real orange," Ben says, admiring his bouquet of flowers. I can't believe he's still holding the flowers. He's moved from sneaking into the movies to petty theft. I think "like father, like son" is close to the truth. But I don't mention that, either. I raise an eyebrow to him.

"Aw, come on, they're not going to miss a handful of flowers," he chuckles. Chuckles!

"And what do you plan on doing with those flowers that you pinched and nearly lost your life for?"

"They're for your ma." Now I stop walking and stare at Ben. That smile creeps back onto his face. "They're for managing to convince you to come to the social. She doesn't need to know we didn't actually get in."

"I would never pick your father over you," I mutter quickly.

Ben hands me the flowers and turns for home.

"Never pick him over anything."

Chapter 12

INTENTIONAL WALK

As long as any fellow's the right type and can make good and get along with other players, he can play ball.
– Frank Shaughnessy, president of the International League

"Joey, Rabbi's waiting for you. Joey?" A hand gently rocks my shoulder and I hear giggling. "Are you asleep?"

I open my eyes to find Shelly standing in front of me. Seeing her first thing is like waking up to a perfect blue-sky day. Her curly reddish-brown hair is pulled back with a headband and she smells like lavender, like one of the soaps we sell at the store.

"Hi," I say. Dumb.

"Hi," she says back, with a laugh.

I smile, embarrassed, and lean over the arm of my chair to pick up my bar mitzvah books. My muscles are stiff, especially my neck.

"If I wait, would you walk me home?" she asks.

HEATHER CAMLOT

Walk Shelly home. Walk Shelly Richter home. Gosh, she's pretty. I could sit here forever and stare at her perfect face. I really could.

"Um … I … yeah … I guess. Okay." Dumb. Dumb. Dumb. I wish I knew how to talk to girls. Ben's got a natural talent for it. Or maybe it's the confidence that comes with looking like Frank Sinatra.

Shelly laughs again and cocks her head in the direction of Rabbi Gottlieb's office. We're going to have a b'nai mitzvah, which is a joint bar and bat mitzvah. Our lessons used to be at the same time, but then Rabbi Gottlieb told us we have to do individual study, "because the date is fast approaching."

I think he decided we have to do individual study because he was fed up with me staring at Shelly, who happens to be his granddaughter. That's how she's even having a bat mitzvah, which is like a bar mitzvah but for girls turning twelve. They're really uncommon. Shelly being Shelly, though, she convinced her grandfather that she had to have one, and I really didn't mind the proposed double ceremony since it meant double the time staring at Shelly. Now I get stared at by Rabbi Gottlieb.

"On to the slaughter." I get up and walk off. *Don't look back*, I tell myself. I know I'll trip or walk into the wall or do something stupid if I look back. Walk Shelly home. Walk—

"Gah!" I looked back.

The door to the office opens and Rabbi Gottlieb gives me a stone-cold stare. I try to smile but it's hard to do when you're on the floor doubled over in pain. I walked right into the sharp-cornered table full of prayer books and *yarmulkes*. Rabbi Gottlieb gives me a hand and leads me into his office. As the door closes, I hear Shelly trying to stifle a laugh.

When I come out an hour later, Shelly's sitting in the same armchair, reading *Nancy Drew: The Clue in the Crumbling Wall.*

"How is it?" I ask, trying to make conversation without sounding—or looking—like a fathead this time.

"More enjoyable than *that* reading," she smiles, pointing to my books.

"Yeah, no kidding. Well, two months left." I don't mention that Rabbi Gottlieb says I'm not working hard enough, so now I have to come twice a week—like I have time for that.

I open the synagogue's front door, only to see Mr. Wolfe across the street, hat tipped, cigarette dangling. He nods at me quickly, then closes his eyes and takes a long drag. He's been following me—synagogue, store, butcher, chicken shop, bank; dozens of places I've spied Mr. Wolfe spying on me. I don't know why he's doing it. I do know butterflies in my gut show up every time I spot him.

Shelly skips down the steps, her curls bobbing up and

down in tune to the clickety-clack of her black and white saddle shoes.

"Oh, I forgot my bat mitzvah notes. I'll be quick." Shelly turns right around and runs back into the synagogue.

"Hey, Joey!"

I guess it was inevitable Mr. Wolfe would call me if I was alone. I cross the street. He relaxes against the triplex, one huge black shoe propped up against the red bricks.

"Geez, kid, you look terrible. Droopy eyelids, pale skin. You not sleeping?"

"You said you were going to tell Ben about you coming around and you never did."

"The time wasn't right," he says in his deep whisper.

"When's it going to be right? Ben got real mad at me."

"Yeah, I heard. I'm sorry, kid. Didn't mean for you to get into any trouble. Thing is, I'm trying to repair my relationship with Ben. It ain't so good, as you know."

"Yeah, I know." I glance at the synagogue steps. Shelly's still inside.

"I'm starting this new business to try to bring us closer together. That's why I don't wanna tell Ben until it's all ready. If it's a success, maybe then he'll have a bit of respect for his old man. That's why I need your help. You know him best."

"I guess."

"You guess!" He laughs and punches me in the arm. I squeeze my eyes and clench my teeth to dull the throbbing pain growing under my shoulder. When I can see again, Mr. Wolfe's got a pleading look. "Can I still count on you?"

Alarms ring in my head, reminding me of Ben's very clear instruction to stay away from his father. But Mr. Wolfe's trying to win Ben back by working real hard on this new business. It's like Jackie Robinson, who's been working real hard to prove himself and win over the haters. And he's got a lot of haters. There've been baseball fans who've threatened to kill him, I mean *really* kill him, just for playing ball in a white league. But Jackie's been succeeding. Maybe Mr. Wolfe will, too. At the very least, it's a real nice thing he's trying to do.

I say yes.

"Thanks, kid!" He's about to punch me again, but I grab my arm and jump back just in time. He roars with laughter and pats my shoulder instead. "Remember, if you need anything, just let me know. And get some sleep!"

As he wanders away with a skip in his step—really, he actually skips—Shelly's back.

"What was that about?"

"Just helping a friend out," I say, feeling really good about myself.

As Shelly and I cross Park Avenue, we head into Outremont.

Shelly's father is a doctor and has lived in Montreal all his life, unlike my pa who came from Russia when he was about my age. Where you're born and when you arrive in Montreal make a huge difference in life. And yet, here I am, walking Shelly home. Into tree-lined, back-yarded, stately homed, picture-postcard Outremont. I'm sure I'm just a curiosity, something foreign from the east side of Park Avenue, which in Montreal might as well be the other side of the world. Girls in Outremont go to Strathcona Academy. It's practically law they don't date boys like me who live on De Bullion and go to Baron Byng.

But I sure like Shelly.

She looks so pretty in her blue-and-white-striped dress. I bet her mom shops at Ogilvy's, this real fancy store downtown. I see the ads in the newspaper all the time. I'm going to take Ma there one day soon.

Walking along Mount Royal Avenue on the west side of Park Avenue, the air smells different. Actually, it doesn't smell at all. No stench of boiled cabbage, gefilte fish, or fried liver and onions. It's like there's some sort of special stink-proof curtain keeping out the cheap food smells that pour out of every kitchen window in my neighborhood. I wonder what people in Outremont eat.

Sandwiches. Everyone eats sandwiches. We should make them at the store, sell them to the people passing by on their way to Fletcher's Field or Mount Royal, or wherever. Nothing fancy, but wrapped up for a picnic to go along with the ice-cold drinks we've been delivering. We can bring some sandwiches in the wagon, too. This is good. This is real good. Business basic #6: Sell complementary products.

"Why are you smiling like that?" Shelly asks with her own smile.

I didn't realize I was smiling but I guess I am. My grin gets bigger. "I just had an idea for the store, that's all."

We turn right off Mount Royal Avenue, make another small right near a weird island, and stop at a pale brown house that seems a little less intimidating than the others nearby, even with its turreted left side, red roof, mix of brick and stone, and breathtaking garden of real orange—

Oh, no. Oh no oh no oh no. It can't be. It just can't. I clutch the stone railing while climbing the steps to the front door. From the corner of my eye, I can see the exact spot where Ben sliced the lilies last night. My stomach twists and I think I'm going to throw up, but that would leave a mess on the lawn, and likely draw attention to the gap in the row of flowers.

"Is it just you and your parents ..." who live in this giant house? I continue in my head and move just a bit to block her view of the garden.

"I have two sisters, Louise and Betty, but Betty, the oldest, won't be here much longer now that she has her M.R.S.," Shelly explains, trying the door, then knocking.

"Her what?" I scrunch my nose and forehead, the way I've seen David do a million times when he doesn't understand something.

"M.R.S. Sounds like a university degree, but it really means Mrs., like Mr. and Mrs. ... a diamond ring on her finger. You never heard that? It's dumb, anyway. The only reason she agreed to go to McGill was to find a husband." She rolls her eyes and sticks out her tongue like it's her turn to throw up. "When I go to university, it will be for a degree. Not a husband."

I snort and quickly cover my mouth. "Sorry," I say, removing my hand, even with Shelly frowning at me. "I'm not laughing at what you said, just the way you said it."

"And how was that?"

"Determined."

"I am."

"Me too."

She smiles and I feel like melting. I walked Shelly home. I walked Shelly Richter home. I wonder what Pa would think of that.

Chapter 13

INTERLEAGUE PLAY

66 *Montreal crowds are as fair and generous as any I've ever seen. But they don't seem to me to be helping Robinson by making that furor over him every time he comes to bat.* **99**
– Bill Reddy, sports editor of the *Syracuse Post-Standard*

"Ah, here's the young man who plans on upstaging my daughter!"

I turn with a start. I never even heard the door open.

"Oh, Papa," Shelly says as she walks around her father and into the house. "Don't mind him, Joey. He likes to tease."

"Okay," I say, her words not making me sweat any less. I wait on the steps. Dr. Richter, at least six feet tall and thin like a tennis player, looks at me strangely.

"Are you waiting for an invitation?" he asks.

"Yes, sir," I say. I know Dr. Richter's known me most of my life, seeing as he's the one we go to at the Herzl Dispensary, the free clinic in our neighborhood. And I know he's seen me with my trousers down and all, but I think I should probably make a better impression. One that doesn't involve him holding a needle near my bare bum while I whimper like a baby.

"Well, how do you like that?" If I'm not mistaken, I think he's impressed. But I could be mistaken.

"Come in, Joey, please." He steps aside to make room.

"Thank you, sir." The inside of the house is even more incredible than the outside, if that's possible. We could fit our flat and the grocery store in here three times over. And the room feels cool. I wonder if they have one of those air conditioners from the States I've been reading about. I follow Dr. Richter into the living room and sit in a real plush striped chair with a pillow that doesn't sag. Shelly and her father sit on the chesterfield, a super-neat stack of *Seventeen* magazines on the coffee table between us.

Then I hear a horribly familiar sound. The growl is low and getting louder. Please, please, please, don't be—

The pit bull runs into the living room and stands at my feet. I'm sure it's getting ready to pounce. I try to get away, but the back of the chair stops me from moving more than a couple of inches. Even dogs don't want me on the west side of Park Avenue.

"Good dog ... good Petey." I try to look and sound calm, even though my heart is beating fast and my skin starts to itch. A repeat of last night. Without the suit. It can't be good to suffer this condition twice in as many days, can it? Maybe I should ask Dr. Richter.

"How did you know his name?" Shelly asks. She moves toward my chair and wraps her arms around the monster.

"Um … just a guess. He's a pit bull. Like the dog in *Our Gang*." Thank you, Ben.

"You've been to the movies?" Shelly asks excitedly. "I've never been."

My face sinks and I see Dr. Richter studying me. "Ah … no," I say, the magazines on the table giving me an idea. "I saw a photo in *Movie Life*. My friend Ben's always showing me his magazines." Shelly nods. Thank you, again.

"Why don't you put Petey in the yard, Shelly? He and Joey don't look very comfortable with each other." What gave it away? The terror in my eyes or the flash of the dog's bone-crushing teeth? Dr. Richter smiles politely and I nod uneasily.

"Petey loves people. Not one aggressive bone in his body," she says, rubbing him along the jaw. "But the fresh air will do him good, won't it, Petey? Not that you didn't get enough of it running out of the house last night. Gave Louise quite a start! She won't be sneaking out again any time soon!" Sneaking out? Who sneaks out with the lights on? No wonder she was caught.

Shelly tugs the dog but he doesn't budge. Except his eyes.

They narrow. I dig my fingers into the padded chair arms. On the third try, she gets him to his feet.

"What's the matter with you?" Petey doggedly stands by the chair, staring at me, like Rabbi Gottlieb. Go figure—they're related. She picks him up and carries him to the back of the house, where I hear a door open and close.

"So how is Baron Byng High School?" Dr. Richter begins, watching me with gray eyes that have a gentleness to them. At least, I hope that's gentleness.

"Good, sir," I say, trying not to break a sweat on their nice chair. What happened to the cool air?

"How did you do last year?"

"Very well, sir. Straight A's."

"Really?" he says, impressed. I think he's impressed. "That's good, keep it up. That will get you into university. Any thoughts on what you'll study?"

My chest constricts, like I'm being cross-examined by one of those movie detectives Ben's always going on about, in a pitch-black room with a light bulb swinging over my head. I haven't even thought about university, never mind what I would study. Lots of kids in my neighborhood never go.

"Oh, Papa, stop interrogating him." Shelly plops back down onto the chesterfield and mouths the words, *I'm sorry*.

I smile and quickly stare down at the Oriental rug under

my feet, not wanting Shelly or her pa to see how red my face must be. There's this white animal on the rug that has a triangle for a body, a rectangle for a beak, really skinny legs, and three long tail feathers, two white, one navy, which makes me think it's supposed to be some sort of exotic bird, like maybe an emu or ostrich. I don't think people should be allowed to walk on these things. They should be hung up like artwork, but the Richters have no room, what with all the paintings already.

"I simply want some details on the man who's stolen ..." Oh, no. Oh no oh no oh no. He was the shadowy figure in the window last night and thinks I'm the one who took off with the flowers. "... my daughter's affection."

Wait, what?

My eyes jolt up and I stare stupidly at Dr. Richter. He's got a mischievous smile on his long face. Shelly groans.

"You're *so* embarrassing." She rolls her eyes and shakes her head.

Dr. Richter has a real wide grin now. He really does like to tease. "So, besides the bar mitzvah lessons, what have you been doing this summer?" He crosses his legs and sits back on the chesterfield, which I notice is the same rust color as the Oriental rug, with spots of navy blue and white. Everything in this house matches, right down to Shelly's and her pa's infectious smiles.

HEATHER CAMLOT

"Working."

"That's it?"

"Yes, sir." I feel like his eyes are drilling into my soul, like he's trying to figure out if I'm good or bad, honest or a liar, sincere or two-faced. I want to break eye contact and concentrate on that emu thing on the rug real badly, but I can't because then he'll figure I'm not worth Shelly's "affection," whatever that means.

"Have you read any books? I'm sure you know we can't pry them out of Shelly's hands." Geez, he asks a lot of questions. I guess it's better than being stared at.

"The newspaper," I answer. "Mostly the business section."

"The business section?"

"Yes, sir."

"Why?"

"Because if I want to get ahead in the business world and control my own destiny, I need to understand everything about it."

He's smiling. I'm not sure if that's good or bad.

"And what is your destiny?"

I look at Shelly. She nods her okay.

"To be rich."

"Well, that's certainly a very wise and noble pursuit."

He's really hard to read. I honestly can't tell if he's impressed or trying not to laugh.

"So you're working at the store, reading the business pages, and going to bar mitzvah lessons. What have you done for fun?"

"Fun, sir?"

He's got that puzzled look again. "Do you mean to tell me you've been on summer holidays for over a month now and you haven't done anything fun? Gone to a baseball game?"

I shake my head.

"Ridden the roller coaster at Belmont Park?"

Another shake.

"He works so hard, Papa. He actually fell asleep at *shul*!" I think Shelly's trying to help me, but I could be mistaken.

"Actually, I fell asleep because I was out late last night," I add quickly.

"Ah, to the big Summer Sunday Social," Dr. Richter says with delight. "So you've had a bit of fun, then, eh?"

"No, sir, I wouldn't say it was fun—"

"My wife helped organize that social," he says.

"She did?" Heart pounding, light bulb blinding. "Well, that's nice, but you see ... um ... I didn't actually get in to—"

"Joey, I'm just kidding. She didn't have anything to do with it. Her parents used to force her to go to those types of parties, too."

"Oh, Papa, Joey's never going to come over again with cruel jokes like that!"

This seems to make Dr. Richter happy. I'm not sure if it's because his joke was a success or he wants me out of the house. "Joey, may I say something?"

"Yes, sir," I manage to squeak out.

He uncrosses his legs, moves up to the edge of the chesterfield, and leans toward me. "You're a kid."

"I'm almost thirteen."

"Do you pay income tax?"

"No, sir."

"Can you vote?"

"No, sir."

"Can you enlist in the army?"

"No, sir."

"Then you're still a kid."

"Papa, leave him alone." Shelly sounds horrified, but her pa doesn't take his eyes off me.

"I know it's not easy without your father, but you need to find time for fun."

You have no idea what I need, Dr. Richter. You want to know what I need? I need money so I can invest it and make more money and get the heck out of the dump my pa abandoned us in. But you could never understand that, not with a big house and an expensive car, and daughters who go to university to find husbands, and enough money to work part-time at a clinic where no one can pay you. But I can't say these things out loud, can I?

"I have a business to make profitable and a family to support," I say. I'm not going to be pushed around or told what to do by someone who knows nothing about me. Okay, he knows a little medical mumbo jumbo about me that he writes down at an appointment every now and then.

He examines me long and hard. I'm trying not to squirm or melt in my plush chair. A sweat stain is really the wrong impression to leave. He sighs, then nods and sits up straight.

"I understand." That's it? And he thinks he understands? I stare at Shelly, possibly for the last time. Petey must know it, too. He runs right back into the room with a smirk instead of a scowl.

"I should be getting home. My brother will be waiting for me to read to him."

"The business section?" I glance at Dr. Richter. He's got an honest smile, but he looks a little sad, like there's something he wants to say but doesn't want to say it. Or he tried to say it, but did it all wrong. That's been pretty much how most folks talk to me and David and Ma now. All I know for sure is the cool air is back and I can breathe again.

"The baseball stats. David can't fall asleep unless he knows how Jackie Robinson's doing," I say. "But then, he's only six."

Chapter 14

HOT STOVE LEAGUE

*❝ This was an adventure in democracy,
an experiment in the sociological laboratory. ❞*
– Sportswriter Dink Carroll

Sometimes being the older brother has its advantages. Like today. As soon as David saw Jackie Robinson's picture in the *Star*, he knew it had to be a big day. He was so wound up about it, he insisted on *schlepping* the grocery wagon to Old Mr. Friedman's so my hands would be free to hold his torn-out news page and read the column out loud. I can definitely get used to people working for me.

"Okay, so the Royals won eight to five over Jersey City. 'Jackie opened last night with a smash against the left-field fence ... Robby broke his bat second time up ...'"

"Whoa ..." David says, tripping over his sneakers, the soles flapping apart from the canvas top.

"'Then came the highlight of the evening when Robinson

out-manoeuvred Bobby Thomson who had him trapped at third base.'"

"Jackie'll get out of it, I know he will!"

"'Robinson went into a football roll, and Thomson pitched over him with the ball.' The writer says there's nothing left for Jackie to prove anymore. We're at Mr. Friedman's."

David runs up the rusted metal stairs while I unload the bags.

"Joey, you read the paper?" Old Mr. Friedman calls from the landing. "One hundred and fifty-six cases of polio disease in Montreal. A crippling menace! Doctors saying the outbreak has nothing to do with location, but seems like an awful lot of kids from here have been heading to the hospital."

"I read it," I say as I reach the door.

"You don't look so good. *Bist krank*?"

"No sir, I'm not sick." I walk past him, through the sweet pineapple smell of David's candy, and into the kitchen. It's faster to put away the groceries than wait for Old Mr. Friedman to stop chit-chatting and let us go. I open the icebox. It's been washed out and organized. Then I notice the wobbly kitchen table doesn't have food-encrusted plates and cutlery on it anymore. I move back into the living room. It smells different. Clean. The small folding table by the decrepit armchair is no longer stacked a mile high with magazines and newspapers. The curtains are open and the whole flat is flooded with light.

I follow a beam of sunlight to the wall that divides the bedroom from the living space and walk over to look at four pictures, each tacked up with two small nails. Pages from a magazine. Old Mr. Friedman's never had anything on his walls, except black bug splats, brown water stains, and long, jagged cracks.

In the first picture, a man is standing with his hands on a bench in front of him; people sitting are looking up at him, listening.

The second has a group of people shown from the neck up, one woman holding prayer beads, another with her hands together near her mouth.

In the third, two kids are being tucked into bed by their ma and pa, who's holding a folded newspaper with the words "Bombings" and "Horror" in the headline.

In the last one, an old woman in an apron with her hair tied back is standing at the head of a nicely set table—all white dishes and white tablecloth and clear water glasses and silver salt and pepper shakers—holding a platter with the biggest turkey I've ever seen. An old man stands behind her, and the rest of the guests are all sitting around the table, talking, smiling.

"The Four Freedoms," says Old Mr. Friedman, making me jump. I didn't think he could sneak up on me, what with all his coughing. "Amazing, eh? Freedom of Speech, Freedom to Worship, Freedom from Fear, and Freedom from Want. Norman Rockwell captured the wartime hopes perfectly."

The people look so real, like I can reach out and actually touch them. "Who's Norman Rockwell?"

"A painter—created these for *The Saturday Evening Post* in 1943. He wanted to do something for the war effort, and being an artist, this was how he thought he could make the biggest impact. He's no *shmegegge*, that one. He was already famous by then, but these … iconic. Doesn't matter what else he's done, what else he'll do, *The Four Freedoms* is his finest accomplishment."

"Where'd you get them?"

"Oh, I've always had them, sitting in one pile or another. But something was smelling rotten so I did a bit of cleaning up. Found a dead rat under some shredded newspaper. Oh, that reminds me …" He turns to David, still standing by the door, still sucking on his candy. "You see that stack of newspapers, *The Sporting News*? For you, if you want. They go back to March … lots of stuff about Jackie Robinson."

"Gee, thanks, Mr. Friedman!" He flips through the first one, a boy on a mission. "Do you have a pair of scissors?"

Mr. Friedman points to a paint-peeling side table by the door, and David beams as he grabs a pair of shiny scissors as long as his arm.

Above the table is a real painting, not one from a magazine.

The paint is thick and layered, with all these violent strokes of blues and blacks and yellows and reds crashing into each other.

"You own a real painting?" I ask stupidly. I mean, it's right there. So, yeah, obviously.

"Sure, why not?" he shrugs.

"Because only rich people own real paintings." People like the Richters and the Bernsteins.

He chuckles. "It's not hard to own a real painting when you paint it yourself."

"Wait. What?" I look from the painting to Old Mr. Friedman. He smiles uncomfortably, then offers me a candy.

"No, thank you."

David comes to stand with us. He scrunches up his face, tilts his head from side to side, and lets out a few little "hmms."

"I like the red." He goes back to his Jackie Robinson project.

Now Old Mr. Friedman starts all-out laughing, then all-out coughing and all-out popping a Life Saver.

"It's amazing, Mr. Friedman. It really is." I let him know like I'm some expert.

"Why?"

"Why? I don't … know. I don't know anything about art." Except that I intend to own lots when I move into Mr. Bernstein's mansion in Westmount.

"You don't need to know anything about art, *boychik*. You think it's amazing. There must be a reason. What was the first thing you thought when you saw it?"

All of a sudden, I feel like I'm back in school, writing a test. He must be reading my mind again because he tells me there are no right answers. No right answers! Every student knows that's even worse!

"I guess I thought, it's not really anything … not like those Norman Rockwell pictures, but it looks so angry."

"*Gut*. And how did it make you feel?"

"Why does that matter?"

"It matters because if art doesn't make you feel, then it's garbage. Pfft." He spits over his shoulder. So much for having cleaned up. "Art is not just some thing to cover empty walls in a Westmount mansion."

How does he always know what I'm thinking? He gives me goosebumps, just like the crashing colors in the painting. Huh. I guess that's my answer.

"It makes the hairs on my arms stand up, like I have the chills."

"*Gut*. I won't throw it in the garbage, then."

"You wouldn't have really done that," I say, more like a question.

"Do you have any more deliveries?" he asks.

"No."

"Then I'll tell you a story. It begins at the end: I haven't painted in years. Not since … well, not much since I arrived here in 1937."

"How come?"

"I needed money to bring my family."

"*You* had a family?" David pipes in.

"Of course," Old Mr. Friedman answers.

"I've never seen them," David continues.

"*Neyn*. They're all dead."

Chapter 15

SACRIFICE HIT

66 Bigotry, race, prejudice and downright ignorance reared ugly heads to harass him at every turn. 99
– Sportswriter Baz O'Meara

"We had a good life in Germany, Gertie and me, and our two daughters, until Hitler decided my art, like Beckmann's, Klee's, Chagall's, was 'degenerate,'" Old Mr. Friedman says. He lowers himself into his no-longer-button-back armchair and stares at his painting above the table.

"What's de … gen … rate?" David asks, climbing onto Old Mr. Friedman's lap.

"It means immoral. But for artists, it meant whatever and whoever Hitler didn't like," Old Mr. Friedman explains.

"I like you."

"Thank you, David. But Gertie, she was scared for my life. She insisted I run far away, get a new life set up for us, and she would follow just as soon as she could. Her parents were old and sick and she didn't want to leave them. The girls didn't want to leave Gertie. I didn't want to leave any of them, but Gertie, you couldn't argue with her ... So, I landed in Canada, which wasn't easy because the country wasn't letting in many Jews, but a couple of people were a real *hilf*." He shifts his focus to me and stares at me funny, giving me those goosebumps again. Goosebumps, in the middle of summer.

"Didn't you miss them?" David asks.

"*Oy*, every day. After the terrible violence of *Kristallnacht*, the 'Night of Broken Glass,' Gertie applied for visa after visa. She and the girls and her parents finally got on a ship heading for Cuba in May 1939, three months before the war broke out, and I don't have to tell you, I breathed the heaviest sigh of relief that day, enough air to fill twenty balloons."

"Whoa ..." David tries to breathe twenty balloons of air.

"But when the ship arrived, they couldn't get off. They sailed north but the United States and Canada wouldn't let them off, either. So the ship turned around and went back to Europe."

"Could they get off the boat there?" David asks, entranced.

"Yes. They went to Belgium."

"Did they like it there?" David asks.

"David!" I shriek. He doesn't understand. But the Holocaust isn't something a six-year-old ought to understand. He looks at me. His eyes are full of fear. His lips quiver. I shouldn't have screamed. I've never screamed at him. I just ... Mr. Friedman ignores the interruption and answers David.

"No. Things weren't good there, David." Old Mr. Friedman wraps him in his arms and carries him into the kitchen. He sets him down at the table, hands him a small glass of milk and a cookie, then picks up the scissors and *The Sporting News* and plunks them on the table for him.

When he comes back to the living room, he returns to his seat, but speaks in a lower voice, so David can't really hear. "A year later, the Nazis invaded Belgium. My family was sent to Auschwitz. Prisoners were starved, tortured, experimented on, and gassed to death. A million people died at the concentration camp, including my Gertie and my girls."

Old Mr. Friedman's eyes get glassy and distant, his cheeks flushed. "I survived, but for what? There's no point in living without family."

I'm not sure what to say or do. I couldn't say or do anything if I wanted to. All this time, I never knew. I never knew Old Mr. Friedman lived alone in this falling-apart house, no one going in or out, because he had no one left. I never knew he brought up every minor newspaper article like it was a sign of World War Three because he lost everything and everyone who meant anything to him in World War Two. I never knew that he knew exactly how Ma feels about losing Pa.

"I picked up a paintbrush out of rage," he points his chin toward the painting over the table and I look at the anger in it again. "I tried to sell my paintings at the newsstand, but people don't buy art during wartime. They steal it. The Nazis walked right into museums and people's homes and grabbed the Klimts and the Raphaels and the Matisses off the walls. I stopped painting for good."

He breathes the deepest breath I've ever heard—though probably not twenty balloons worth—then looks at me, sitting cross-legged on the floor.

"*The Four Freedoms, boychik.* Speech, Worship, Fear, Want. President Roosevelt had hope for the future. So did your pa." He grips both arms of his chair and pushes himself to standing. He walks over to the table, looks up at his painting, then opens the drawer and pulls out the grocery bill.

"It's only August 10, Mr. Friedman."

"It's all right. I got it. You take it." He closes my hand around the money.

"Thank you." I'm not sure what else to say or do. Again.

He heads to the kitchen and taps David on the shoulder to let him know it's time to go, picks up the stack of *The Sporting News*, and places it securely in his arms. David and I file out of the flat.

"You boys are my family now," Old Mr. Friedman whispers.

When I turn back to say—I don't know what—the door is shut.

David and I don't say a word as we walk down the stairs. I came here delivering the groceries. I'm leaving with a very clear picture of how sick and twisted the world can be. Our dump of a neighborhood may be a ghetto, but it's not that kind of ghetto. We're safe here. As I pull the wagon off the patch of dirt, I notice the curtains in Old Mr. Friedman's have been closed.

Chapter 16

SCREAMING LINE DRIVE

66 There have been times during the past season when the pressure was so great on Robbie that he almost collapsed under it. 99
– Sportswriter Dink Carroll

SEPTEMBER 1946

The hospital waiting room is so white. Except for the black frame of the clock on the wall across from where I'm sitting. Ticking off how long we've been sitting here. Ticking off how long before we hear anything. Tick. Tick. Tick. It's like a bomb ready to go off.

I'm like a bomb ready to go off.

Life's been pretty routine for the last three weeks. Then an hour ago, after delivering groceries, David and I walk into the store. One minute Ma's sweeping the floor, the next she's sweating like crazy, clutching her heart like it's going to explode, unable to catch her breath, shaking, like she was dropped into the Arctic. Her knees crumple and she crashes to the floor. Then silence.

We don't hear the wailing of the ambulance. I'm yelling, David's yelling—at Ma, to get up, to wake up. I don't know who called for the ambulance—Ben? A customer?—but it brings her here, to the Royal Victoria Hospital. On the west side of Park Avenue. Not to Hotel Dieu, on the east side. I guess getting real sick is the quick ticket across. Great. Swell.

The hospital staff won't let us see Ma, what with the polio outbreak going strong—I'm surprised they even let us in the hospital—but they say the episode's passed. Episode? What does that mean? Radio has episodes, like *Dick Tracy* and *The Green Hornet*. Does this mean this is part of a series, that it'll happen again?

"Joey."

I groggily roll my head at my name. David's snuggled in my lap. He's asleep. Better that he's asleep. Shelly's pa sits down in the chair next to me.

"Is she going to die?" I feel like I'm on an airplane about to crash. And I have no parachute.

"No, no. I've seen her and I've met with the physician. She's recovering well," Dr. Richter says, patting the part of my leg not covered by David.

"Did she have a heart attack like Pa? It looked like a heart attack."

"It wasn't a heart attack."

The hairs on the back of my neck feel sticky.

"Is this the first time you've seen this happen to her?" he asks.

I nod.

"Does she sleep?"

I shake my head. The shaking and nodding remind me how sore my neck's been lately. I roll my head around and hear cracking.

"No sleep at all?"

I've been so busy with the store and the side businesses and with lessons and with Shelly and with David and with Ben that I haven't really noticed. I should have noticed. I should have noticed how much she's been in the store and how often she's been in that God-awful robe. I shrug.

"When did the fatigue start?"

I look down at my shoes. The leather is worn through, the toes all white where they used to be brown.

"Since your father's death?" he asks.

I nod.

"Have you ever seen her tremble, breathe rapidly, or sweat profusely?"

"Only today."

It's his turn to nod. He takes a deep breath and leans back in the chair.

"I found lots of Aspirin in the linen closet," I blurt out. Like that's supposed to mean something.

"Does she complain a lot about headaches?"

"She doesn't complain about anything."

He smiles and little laugh lines form around his mouth and eyes. I feel more awful than ever. She should have complained. We could have prevented this ... this ... whatever this is.

"How about pains in her chest?"

"You said it wasn't a heart attack!"

"It wasn't. Her heart is perfectly fine. Broken but healthy."

"What does that mean? My pa's dead and now he's trying to kill Ma?" David wakes up to my loud voice, wraps his arms around my neck, then snuggles back in. I don't want to get angry in front of David, in front of Dr. Richter, in front of anyone. My fists ball up and it's getting harder to see.

"Are you going to tell me what's wrong with her?" I demand. I'm tired of the questions. I'm tired of waiting. I'm tired of that stupid ticking clock. I just want to go to sleep and never wake up. But I can't. Ma and David depend on me. I have to take care of them. "I'm not a kid. I can take it," I say.

He looks at that time-bomb of a clock.

"Keep in mind that I am not a psychiatrist, nor have I had the chance to speak with any type of specialist yet."

"Okay. Fine."

"It looks to me like a form of anxiety neurosis."

"What's that?"

"Well, from what I understand, it's a state of panic. A stressful experience, like the death of a loved one, financial loss, business worry—all these things can trigger fear and anxiety in a person, and some have gone so far as to say it can lead to agoraphobia—"

"What's that?"

"Fear of going outdoors."

I think she has that. She hardly ever leaves the flat or the store. Does she ever leave? Maybe she's afraid to leave. Leave us, like Pa. Like if she goes, she won't come back. Except the exact opposite just happened, didn't it? Her not leaving almost made her leave us. My head hurts.

"So Ma's gone crazy?" I wonder if it runs in the family, because I think I'm going crazy, too. How many bad things can happen to one family? Really, I'd like to know. My fists tighten against David's back. Dr. Richter takes one of my clenched hands and laces his fingers through mine. I look into his gray eyes and see kindness. I'm burning up with sadness, madness.

"So how do we fix it?" I ask through gritted teeth.

"I have to do some research. Sounds like we caught it early

so we may be able to avoid sedatives. But we have to work on the stress she's feeling. Joey ..." He stops a minute to study me. Irritate me.

"How are you feeling?"

"Fine."

"How many businesses are you running?"

That's an odd question. I look at the clock and start counting on my fingers:

1. The store
2. The delivery service
3. The popsicles—but that's dying with the change of weather
4. The ice-cold drinks at the mountain and park—that one's dying, too
5. The picnic sandwiches—another potential goner for the season.

I lift my other hand and raise another finger.

6. The gardening. I haven't actually started this one yet, but I've been doing a lot of reading—I bet Dr. Richter knows, since Shelly lent me her ma's books. The plan is to go year-round, gardening in the spring and summer, leaf-raking in the fall, and snow removal in the winter. Wait, does that count as two more businesses? Seven. Eight. I'm sure it will be a

hit in Outremont, and it falls into business basic #7: Diversify—expand into new areas of business.

9. Ma's *rugelach*. This is also business basic #7. The cookies are doing real well—the smell is irresistible and the way she rolls the dough into little moons and sprinkles just a bit of icing sugar on them, no customer can resist all that cinnamon melt-in-your-mouth goodness. We leave them on the counter with a sign that says Grosser's Goodies and ... oh, no. Oh no oh no oh no. I made Ma anxious. I asked her to bake the rugelach because I knew they'd be a hit. I've been making her work too much and now she's gone crazy from it.

"Joey." Dr. Richter pulls me away from my counting and planning, and folds up my hands. "That's a lot of fingers. How long have you had that rash on your face and the bags under your eyes?"

"I don't know. Why?"

"And besides the neck tension and irritability—"

"My mother's in the hospital!"

"And angry outbursts—is anything else bothering you?" He looks concerned. Why does he look concerned?

"No." I decide not to tell him about Mr. Wolfe.

"You have enough symptoms to land yourself in the

hospital if you're not careful."

"I'M NOT—" I start to yell, then remember what he said about the angry outbursts. "I'm fine."

"It's okay to feel under pressure and to work toward a goal, Joey. But it's not okay to ignore when the pressure gets to be too much and not take care of yourself."

"I—"

"I know you've been reading the sports pages. Have you noticed how many times the word 'pressure' is near Jackie Robinson's name? He didn't sit out those three games last week after clinching the pennant just to nurse his bumps and bruises. I bet you he was taking the time to try to recover from the constant abuse and stress he's been under all season. It's grueling on the body and the mind. No one can go on like that."

"But—"

"No one," he cuts me off again. "They stumble and fall. Even the greats. But then they pick themselves up, brush themselves off, and get right back in the game. Usually, hopefully, a lot stronger and wiser. Jackie did. Your mother will. The question is, what will you do?"

I don't plan on falling, so there's no point in answering.

"You have nine businesses according to your fingers. Drop eight of them."

"I can't do that. I need to—"

"Get ahead in the business world and control your own destiny."

"Yes. And I have—"

"A business to make profitable and a family to support."

His cutting in is really annoying.

"I understand, Joey. I really do. But let me tell you something. You're not going to reach your destiny or support your family if you continue along this road."

"And what road is that?" I ask, not enjoying this conversation one bit. It's a fatherly conversation. And he is not my father.

"You're working yourself to death."

I can't believe he actually said that. I don't think he believes he actually said it, either, because he rubs his face in his hands really hard, drags them down his neck, and stares up at the ceiling for a few seconds. I can see the red lines his fingers made all the way along. When he finally looks at me, all I see is judgment. I feel as clammy and sweaty as the day Shelly invited me over. I'd definitely take Rabbi Gottlieb's stare over this any day. Maybe even the dumb dog's stare and drooling scowl.

"I'm going to go look into the bill and then I'll drive you and David home," he says, real calmly.

"No!" I'm not sure where that came from, but there's no way I'm taking money from him. From anyone. No credit.

"Can you afford the hospital fee?"

"I'll figure something out."

"Let me—"

"No, I'll figure it out!"

"Take a week and let me know what you come up with. Otherwise, I'm happy to pay it." He pats me on the shoulder, messes David's hair, and moves toward the door.

"Can we take Ma home?"

"Not right now. I'll drive her when she's discharged."

"Okay," I mumble. "Thank you for coming." I can hardly hear me. I quickly glance up to see Dr. Richter nod and leave.

How in the world are we going pay for this?

Chapter 17

LOCK HIM UP

*❝ The more successful he is, the more certain
he is to encounter tough opposition. ❞*
– Sportswriter Baz O'Meara

The newspapers always talk about how people ought to save money for a rainy day, like if they lose their job and stuff like that. Pa got David and me those piggy banks from the Montreal Capital and Commerce Bank so we could save for the future. David's going to have to save for the future on his own. My West of Park Avenue Fund has officially become the rainy day fund to pay for Ma's hospital bill.

I drag the gleaming silver box out from under my bed, then head to Ma's room to find Pa's matching bank. I doubt he'll mind me using the money—it's not like he needs it.

I peek my head around the doorframe. Ma's eyes are closed. Her breathing is soft and slow and she's looking real peaceful all curled up in her robe under a cozy wool blanket.

Along the foot of the bed is another blanket, the one Ma knitted by herself. It's the ugliest thing ever. The pattern—if you can call it a pattern—is all uneven and you can see all the knots from where she ran out of yarn and, if you open it right up, you can see the sides are not even close to being straight. Ma thinks it's the ugliest thing, too, but it was the first time and last time she ever knitted anything, and Pa insisted all the work she put into it made it beautiful. He was wrong. It's still ugly. But I get why she keeps it.

I tiptoe past and open the closet—Pa's clothes are still hanging there—and I find the box in a corner on the floor, covered in a thick layer of dust. I try to blow it off, but not one particle moves. I rub the box with my fingers. It feels sticky, like grimy glue that hasn't completely dried. It's bumpy, too. Curled up beetle carcasses. Great. Swell.

After I've waited in line forever at the Montreal Capital and Commerce Bank, the teller opens my box with a special key and hands over what little I have in there. I could have sworn there'd be more. When I pass her Pa's box, she looks like she's ready to throw up. I guess I should have cleaned it first.

"I'm sorry, but our records show this bank box doesn't belong to you." She wraps her hand in a linen handkerchief and takes hold of the box's metal handle.

"It's my pa's and he's dead. Your records must show that."

"I'm afraid our records do not say anything of the kind. Your mother will need to come to the bank and present the death certificate. Then this box may be opened," she says, all grouchy, like suddenly I'm a fly she can't swat.

"She can't come to the bank. She's not well and I need whatever's in here to pay the hospital bill." I'm trying not to get angry or have a crazy outburst. All I need is for Dr. Richter to walk into the bank and say I told you so.

"Without proper authorization, I cannot help you."

I reach for the box, but she grips the handle harder. Her red hair falls in her face. She uses her other hand to remove the strands stuck to her red lipstick.

"You really think I'm going to walk out of here without this box? I brought it. Let. Go." Her red painted fingers slip away. I hope the dead bugs stick to the handkerchief and never wash off. I grab Pa's box from the counter and mine from the marble floor and storm out of the bank. I run the eight blocks home, but I stay on Roy. I don't want to turn onto De Bullion. I don't want to go inside. I don't want to see Ben or David or Ma or anyone. Unless they have a way of unlocking Pa's box. Frustrated, I drop my box on the ground and throw Pa's against the store's brick wall.

Brick wall.

I pick up the metal box and throw it against the wall again.

And again. And again. On the eleventh pounding, it splits open. Not a cent falls out. Not a cent. Just some paper. I knew there was no change in the box; it would have been heavier. It would have clinked and clanked when I shook it. I pick up the piece of paper. Torn-out newsprint with some stock prices from January 1933. Eight months before I was born.

Nothing. My father has nothing. Not a single plan for a rainy day.

I grab the box and smash it against the wall. Again. And again. Not caring one bit about the blood trickling down my knuckles and along the back of my hand.

"You can have mine, Joey." David's standing at the corner of the store. Close enough to feel my anger. Far enough to not be slashed by flying metal. I close my eyes, take a deep breath, and slide down the brick wall to the ground.

"You keep your money, David. You keep it real close and never let anyone take it from you." I wipe my nose on my sleeve.

"It's okay. I don't need it."

"Yes, you do. You're just too young to know it." David sits down next to me, so close our sides touch.

"Ma's gonna be okay," he says, the little adult that he is.

"Of course she will," I whimper, the big kid that I am.

"You're gonna be okay, too." He looks up at me with those deep brown eyes and squeezes my hand. I drop my head onto his, my cheek resting on his stick-straight hair. My head feels so heavy. I feel so heavy.

"David?"

I hear Ben's voice. He pops his head around the corner and sees us against the wall. "Hey Joey, you're back. How'd it go?"

"Not so good."

"Oh. Well, your ma's awake and looking for David. Something about cutting up the tablecloth while cutting out pictures in the newspaper."

David flashes his I'm-too-cute-to-be-yelled-at look and, with head and shoulders drooping, shuffles into the store, like a condemned man on his way to the electric chair. He'll be lucky if he gets off that easy.

"Should I ask how many tablecloths he's gone through?" Ben asks, grinning.

"Probably not."

"You comin' in? I'm thinking of building a pyramid out of cans of tomatoes for the window. Upside down."

I want to laugh but I just can't. "Soon," I say.

Ben nods, smiles like he understands, and goes back in. Maybe he does understand. I don't know. He never says anything, unless it's about Hollywood, and then he can't stop talking. But most days, he just comes and helps out at the store, in between eating boxes of Cracker Jack and reading

Movie Life. He says he likes the peace and quiet. Between his chatter about the movies and David's about baseball, I have no idea what peace and quiet he's talking about. Here, sitting against the brick wall, no one passing by, this is peace and quiet. I can get used to peace and quiet.

"What a lovely picture. I wish I had a camera." Mr. Wolfe is standing on the sidewalk, far enough away from the corner to not be seen through the store windows. He lights a cigarette, takes a long drag, and lets out a thin line of gray smoke. His fingers are stained with nicotine. "Business must be booming if you have time to take a break," he says with a slip of a smile.

"I can't talk to you," I say, pushing up against the wall.

"Did I do something to hurt your feelings?" He takes his hat off and holds it against his chest apologetically.

I roll my eyes. "No, you didn't hurt my feelings. It's just— look, we can't talk here. Ben's inside. Let's ... let's just go around the block or something." I know Mr. Wolfe's plan is for the greater good and all, but I don't want to destroy my friendship with Ben along the way.

"You're right." He pops his hat back on and follows me, keeping a couple of feet back. "Am I far enough back?" he calls out. "I don't want to risk Ben seeing us together."

I roll my eyes again. I seem to be doing that a lot lately. I turn the corner and wait the thirty seconds it takes for him to catch up. "Have you explained things to Ben yet?"

"No." He takes a quick a drag on his cigarette.

"Are you even planning on telling him? I don't like keeping things from him," I say, annoyed.

"How's your mother?" The old change-of-subject trick. Mr. Wolfe has officially closed the conversation about Ben. Great. Swell.

"She's getting better. Thank you for asking." My eyes dart around as I try to see if anyone is watching or listening in. Anyone being Ben. I shouldn't be here. I hate that I'm here. But what am I supposed to do? Mr. Wolfe's looking particularly dark this afternoon, all heavy eyebrows and gray skin, and I don't like the way he's cracking his knuckles between sucks on the cigarette. I wonder if he's worried about his gambling business now that the police Morality Squad is going after gambling dens and horse-betting places. I wonder if his new business idea is still going to happen. I need the money. Badly.

"How are the credits? All paid up?" he asks, blowing a series of smoke rings in my direction. The smell makes my eyes burn.

"Almost."

"The Abelsons are a real pain in the neck, eh?"

"How do you know it's the Abelsons?" A shiver runs through me. Make that a quake. He shouldn't know stuff like that about the store. I stare at him hard like that will make him crumble and tell all, but Mr. Wolfe just grunts and watches his swirls of smoke.

"I make it my business to take care of the people my family associates with." A lopsided smile crosses his face. "Ben associates with you, so I'm taking care of you."

"What does that mean?"

"It means I paid your ma's hospital bill."

"What?"

"I paid the hospital bill. It's the least I could do after all your family has done for Ben."

"I don't give credit and I don't take credit," I say matter-of-factly.

"That's good business sense. I'm proud of you. But what's important is your ma gets better and you have a roof over your heads and you stop smashing innocent little piggy banks. When the time comes to return the favor, I'll let you know." He remembers the cigarette in his mouth and takes another drag. I wonder if he single-handedly keeps the Bernsteins in business with all his smoking. He looks at his gold watch, then down the street. "I gotta go. Keep your nose clean." He lowers the brim of his hat and dashes off toward Park Avenue.

What kind of favor does he have in mind?

Chapter 18

STAYED ALIVE

❝ *There isn't any doubt of his capacity.* **❞**
— Sportswriter Baz O'Meara

I run back to the store, tear open the door, and bolt inside. And smash right into Mr. Abelson, sending him flying to the ground.

"Geez, Joey!" Ben calls out as he comes round the counter to help.

"I'm so sorry, Mr. Abelson! I didn't see you. Here … let me help you." I reach out a hand and he takes it, Ben holding him from the back.

"*A sheynem dank*, boys, thank you very much." Mr. Abelson steadies himself with a hand against the top of a shelf and takes several wheezy gasps of air to settle his shakes. He looks pretty sharp in a new three-piece suit.

"How is your mother?" Mr. Abelson asks when he recovers. Ben takes his arm and leads him to the counter real slowly.

"She's getting better, sir. Thank you for asking," I say for the second time today.

"And look at you! Taking care of business, eh? Just a month until the bar mitzvah now. A man soon enough." He straightens his paisley tie and flattens what's left of his hair. He looks like he wants to ask one of us out on a date, all gawky and nervous. Ben cracks a kind smile, and David, standing next to him, does the same.

"Mrs. Abelson would have come herself, but she's been pulling in quite a bit of sewing and mending work and didn't feel she could spare the time. In any case, while we are both so thankful, it was a lovely excuse for me to come and thank you personally for your generosity and understanding."

After patting the pockets of his jacket and slacks, he lets out a hushed "Aha!"—thrilled with whatever he just discovered—and takes out a ratty, brown leather billfold. He opens it, removes a thick wad of cash, and slips it across the counter to me. David's eyes look like they're gonna pop out of his skull. Bet mine do, too.

"We've been keeping an exact tab of what we owe you and this is the complete sum," Mr. Abelson says proudly. "I was recently hired by the Montreal Capital and Commerce Bank. I'm in training, and when they say I'm ready, they'll move me to a permanent position." Mr. Abelson's chest actually puffs out and the biggest grin spreads across his face, the kind of grin that makes you smile, too, whether you want to or not.

"That's great news!" I reply. "And thank you for the payment." Ben shakes Mr. Abelson's hand and congratulates him on the new job. As he marches back to the door, I quickly count out the money and put it in the wall safe hidden behind a tin Coca-Cola sign, which is more decoration than protection. Pa just didn't like looking at the safe. He did like looking at the sign.

"You should go to the bank with all that," Ben says, watching me.

"Yeah. But I have some suppliers to pay first." Everyone's paid up. Everyone's made good.

"*Oy vey*, I almost forgot," says Mr. Abelson. "Mrs. Abelson said I would forget and I nearly did." He zips back, raising and shaking a bag he's been carrying. He puts it on the counter and pulls out three sets of hats, scarves, and mitts, in pink, black, and blue.

"Mrs. Abelson's been knitting these as a thank-you. I know it's too warm to think about winter yet, but it will come soon enough." He turns to David and hands him the blue set. "I'm supposed to tell you that this blue is the exact same shade as on the Montreal Royals uniform." He winks at David, who squashes up the left side of his face to wink back but, as hard as he tries, only manages a goofy blink. Mr. Abelson claps his hands together and chuckles.

"How much would she charge for a set?" I ask.

"Oh, I'm not sure. Why?" Mr. Abelson replies, looking confused. Well, more confused than usual.

"They're real nice. Would Mrs. Abelson think about selling them here?" Business basic #8: Take over another business.

"Well, that's a lovely idea."

"Can you ask her to come see me? Maybe we can work out a deal."

"Always taking care of business! I will certainly let Mrs. Abelson know." He waves goodbye and heads out the door.

I grab some of the cash out of the safe. "I'm gonna run to the bakery to pay up and restock," I tell Ben, who nods and starts reading David the sports page. Out the door, I turn the corner from De Bullion to Roy and find Mr. Wolfe standing there. Like he knew I'd come out.

"All paid up now?" he smirks.

"Yeah," I answer hesitantly.

"The Abelsons really are a pain in the neck."

"How'd you know?"

"That he was coming to pay or that he has a new job?"

"Both."

"I told you, kid, I make it my business to take care of the

people my family associates with." This is the exact same conversation as twenty minutes ago. But so much has happened in those twenty minutes. So much that he knows and I don't.

"What's Ben got to do with Mr. Abelson?"

Mr. Wolfe takes a long look at me, then punches me in the shoulder, forcing me to stumble and hit the store's brick wall. Against my bloody knuckles. I never see those punches coming.

"That's a good one, kid," he laughs. "You had me going."

I have no idea what he's talking about. The only time I've ever heard Ben even mention the Abelsons was when he asked for Adele at the party at Mr. Bernstein's mansion.

"I let a banker friend pay off his gambling debt by giving Abelson a job. Then I reminded Abelson to pay you back." A jolly grin spreads across his chubby face, like a Jewish Santa Claus.

"I didn't know you had friends at the bank."

"Why would you?" He's got a point. "Be smart and lock up all that money."

"Yes, sir." I hurry to the bakery, pay our bill, and stroll back to the store, feeling good. Thanks to Mr. Wolfe, the store isn't owed money and the store doesn't owe money.

But I still owe Mr. Wolfe.

Chapter 19

PINCH HITTER

❝Robinson has squared accounts and all is well.❞
— Sportswriter Lloyd McGowan

Stupid polio epidemic. I was really hoping it would postpone the first day of school by at least a month. But we started back today, so all we got was two lousy weeks. That makes two weeks and two days since Ma's "episode." Two weeks and one day since Mr. Wolfe took care of the hospital bill and our last credit was paid. Two weeks to the day since the robberies started.

Robberies. In my neighborhood. Honestly, who's dumb enough to rob poor people? What's even the point? The thief can't be stealing enough to live on. And it's just wrong. I mean, yeah, obviously stealing is wrong and illegal and all that, but if you're going to steal, you should steal from the rich and give to the poor, like Robin Hood. It's just so obvious.

HEATHER CAMLOT

Anyway, between worrying about a robbery, running the store, working on my other money-making strategies, caring for a mother who thinks she's recovered from her "episode," and practicing for my bar mitzvah, I haven't had much time for myself. Rabbi Gottlieb says I'm his worst student ever. Aren't people of God supposed to be positive and encouraging?

SLAM!

After nearly shattering the glass of the store door, David storms over to where I'm restocking the shelves. I've had no time for him, either.

"Can we go to Fletcher's Field?"

"I have to work, David," I say.

"Ah, applesauce. No one's even here."

"I still can't go. It was Ma's first full day back in the store and she needs to rest. I can take you to the park if you want. If we run, it shouldn't be more than fifteen minutes to go and come back."

"It's no fun without you. You don't play with me anymore."

"I don't have time."

"Pa would take me! He'd have time!" Pa wouldn't take him. He'd be working. "Pa said you have to take care of me!"

"I'm trying to make us money."

"Pa never cared about making money!"

"Yeah, and he's dead and we have nothing!" I feel my face get red and my body burn with anger. It doesn't take much to set me off these days. "I have to take care of you by getting us money and getting us out of this dump so we can have a real life. I'm going to do it, too, just like I said. Over with the rich folks on the west side of Park Avenue!" David stares at me, his eyes full of tears, then he runs behind the counter.

"Who cares about rich folks! Jackie Robinson lives on the east side! Mr. Friedman told me so! If Jackie can live here, why can't we?" he yells back, then ducks down.

Thump ... thump ... thump ... thump ... David is in his hiding spot, tossing a ball against the lower half of the wall that he's plastered with Jackie Robinson newspaper clippings. I join him behind the counter. He's got a new cartoon with a large drawing of Jackie Robinson holding a bat over one shoulder, and there are all these boxes reporting what a great year the Royals have had and the records they've broken, like the club winning a hundred games, like Marv Rackley's sixty-five stolen bases, like Jackie being the first Royal to win the International League batting crown, and a bunch more. Nice to know someone's having all the luck, because it sure isn't us. David's catching the white ball in a new glove.

"Where'd you get those from?" I ask.

"From Ben," he snaps.

"And the cartoon? It's not from the *Star*."

"From Mr. Friedman. It was in the *Gazette*."

"Why all the gifts?" I ask.

"Why not? You don't think I deserve them?" He doesn't even bother looking at me.

"I don't know. What did you do to deserve them?" He starts pounding the ball against the wall and, though it's hurtling back at him, he's got real good coordination for a kid his—

Oh, no. Oh no oh no oh no! It's David's birthday.

"What's the matter with me? Of course you deserve them. You're seven today!" He stops tossing the ball and looks up at me, his mouth a tight line. What I wouldn't give to see his loopy grin. But all I get is this real intense examination, like he's seeing me for the first time, realizing who I am. I didn't know I could feel worse than just a second ago. I can.

"Yeah, I am." He stares back at the wall and starts tossing the ball again, but a bit lighter.

"David, I'm real sorry. I forgot your birthday. I'll make it up to you, promise." Look at me, please look at me. He doesn't.

"You been working real hard to make money. It's okay." I pass the honesty test. But my gut is churning fast.

"It's not okay. We'll go play ball, David—we'll go tomorrow, okay? I'll ask Ma to watch the store a little longer. And then maybe you can take her for a walk. She should be getting out more. What do you think?"

He doesn't say a word.

I leave his hiding place and step outside. I close my eyes, lean against the window, and breathe in deeply. The air smells vinegary, like rotting apples, and I can hear the clomping of a horse and the creaking of the ice cart getting louder. I don't bother looking. I don't feel like being nice. Nice gets you nowhere and nothing. As the nasty odor of horse poop mixed with wet hay trails away, a new smell takes over. Lavender. I open my eyes to see Shelly standing next to me.

"What's the matter with you?" She nudges me with her arm. My stomach bubbles like acid when I see how happy she looks.

"Nothing." Except that I'm a cruddy brother.

"Is David inside? I have a present for him."

"How'd you know it was his birthday?"

"You told me last week. Don't you remember? You said your birthdays are less than two weeks apart so you usually celebrate together, but because of the bar mitzvah this year ..."

"I did?" I roll my head her way, completely puzzled by what she's saying. When she realizes I'm not kidding, she stops smiling. Fast.

"You forgot David's birthday?" She checks my face for some sign of teasing. "You're working too hard."

"My pa would never have forgotten David's birthday."

She looks at me.

"What?"

"I just … I've never heard you mention your father since …"

I want to say he's not worth mentioning, but I know that's not gonna go over well.

"You take it and give it to David," she says, offering me the package.

"What is it?" I ask, doubtful it would make any difference.

"A baseball hat from the Royals," she says.

I straighten up against the window and stare into her eyes to see if she's the one teasing now.

"How'd you get that?"

"Boy, you ask a lot of questions for someone in the doghouse." She tries to get me to smile, but I'm not taking the bait. "One of the players is Papa's patient. He gave it to my father, my father gave it to me, and now I'm giving it to you to give to your brother."

Now I know why Dr. Richter knew so much about what was going on in the ballpark, and about what Jackie was doing during his three days off, when he lectured me at the hospital about pressure. I press back against the glass.

"You should give it to him."

"I should, but I'm not going to." She stuffs the package in my folded arms.

"Thank you, Shelly."

She smiles. It really is an infectious smile.

Chapter 20

PRODUCTIVE OUT

*❝So far he has carried the torch for his race
with magnificent dignity. ❞*
— Sportswriter Baz O'Meara

"Why do you look so mad, Joey?" David asks, standing on his tiptoes and pushing his Royals baseball cap up and away from his eyes, all the better to see into the cookie jar.

"I have to redo my book report."

He pulls out one of Ma's famous *rugelach*, studies it, tosses it back in, and takes another. Ma's been baking up a storm since the "episode." I told her to forget about selling the cookies, but she said baking relaxes her, whatever that means, and if she's going to be baking anyway, making extra for the store wasn't any bother. She has been looking pretty relaxed lately. She even went for a walk with Old Mr. Friedman yesterday.

"How come?" David shakes his head at the latest cookie and tries again.

HEATHER CAMLOT

"Eh?"

"How come you gotta redo your book report?"

"I didn't do well." So much for those straight A's I told Dr. Richter about.

"How come?" Holding what I'm guessing is the biggest *rugelach* in the jar, he steps back down and slides onto a chair. He wriggles around, trying to get comfortable against the spindly back but, instead, one of the posts loosens out of its hole. He puts down his cookie and pops the post back in.

"I don't know why I didn't do well. Nah, actually, I do. I think *The Red Pony* is a stupid book."

David picks up my copy of *The Red Pony* lying on the dining table. "How come?"

"Because it's one hundred pages of boring baloney about death and disappointment and a mean kid who only thinks about himself."

"Huh. So what happens?" he asks, concentrating on the cover, like it holds all the answers.

"A boy gets a pony."

"That's it?"

"No. The pony dies."

"The boy must have cried a lot."

"Actually, he killed a bird."

"How come?"

"Because he was real angry about the pony."

"Ma cried when Pa died," he says, eating the tips of the moon-shaped cookie.

"Yeah."

"What about Mr. Friedman? He didn't cry when he told us about his family. You think he killed a bird?"

"I don't think Mr. Friedman is capable of killing a bird." I scan all the red marks on my paper. This is going to take forever to rewrite. We only got ten days to read the dumb book and write the dumb report because the teacher wanted to make up for the late school start.

"'Cause he's old?"

"No, because he's ... I don't know ... he's nice. Mr. Friedman just ... he stays to himself. I've never seen him leave home except for work and that walk with Ma the other day, and I've never seen anyone visit him."

"We visit."

"Yeah. We do."

"Maybe that's why he doesn't cry."

"Maybe," I say, chewing the top of my pencil.

"I cried when Pa died," he says, less a reminder and more like a statement of fact.

"Yeah, you did."

"I never saw you cry. Did you cry like me?" He drops the

book on the table.

"No," I say matter-of-factly.

"You musta done something."

This is a really big conversation for such a little kid, and I don't want to be having it.

"Whatdja do?"

"I—" I tilt my head and look at the living room wall, focusing on nothing in particular. There's nothing on the wall to look at except a real long crack that I should get around to patching. "Huh," I mutter with a small laugh, then turn back to David. "Actually, I killed a bird."

"You killed a bird? How could you, Joey?"

"Well, not exactly a bird."

"A squirrel? An ant?"

"No—"

"A rat? A rat would be okay, Joey, so that it doesn't eat my ears."

"I didn't kill a rat, David."

"Then what, Joey? Tell me."

"I killed a piggy bank." I smile uncontrollably, maybe maniacally, while watching David try to make sense of what I just said. I start giggling. I can't help it. David looks at me like maybe I've lost my mind. Maybe I have. A smile flashes across his face quicker than you can say "Jackie Robinson."

"Yeah, yeah! I saw that. The bank box did kinda fly like a bird!" he giggles.

"Like a bird crashing into a brick wall!" I roll up a piece of yesterday's newspaper sitting on the table and throw it at the crack in the living room wall.

"I thought you were going to break the store, Joey, I really did!" he says, laughing, tearing up and tossing his own piece of newspaper. We attack the paper, competing to see who can throw the most. My face hurts from all the smiling. We run to the wall and grab as many balls of paper off the floor as we can, then race back to the table and start throwing again in a frenzy.

"Ahem," Ma says dryly.

David and I stop mid-throws, arms still in the air. She's standing in the doorway. The one in the living room wall. Balls of newspaper at her feet.

"I thought David might want today's paper." She holds it out for him to take. He drops his balled-up pieces and hotfoots it over to her, takes the paper, and flips right to the sports section.

"Whoa ..."

I look over his shoulder to see all the press the Royals got for winning their second Governor's Cup title.

"I see you're working hard." She kicks a couple of the newspaper balls by her feet and flashes me her ready-to-take-on-the-world smile. At least I know she's not upset. Actually, if I didn't know better, I'd say she'd like to throw a few herself. Maybe I'll leave some on her bed when I clean up later. Just to see.

"We were just having some fun."

"Good. You need to find time for fun." Great. Swell. Same words Dr. Richter said to me at Shelly's house. Why do I get the feeling his visits haven't only been about checking on Ma?

We go down to the store, leaving David trying to decode the sports column that he'll ask me to read before bed.

Ma picks up the broom and sweeps the spotless floor.

"You look nice, Ma." Her hair is in a bun and she's out of that awful robe and wearing a navy dress.

"Thank you, dear." She sweeps up the invisible pile of dirt.

"I figured it out," I say, sitting down on Ben's overturned crate.

"The meaning of life?"

"What? No."

"How to make a hundred dollars a week?"

"Still working on that."

"Hmm ... how to get your brother to eat a vegetable?"

"No one can figure that out."

She smiles. "I give up, what did you figure out?"

"*The Red Pony*."

"Ah. Did you take your teacher's advice and put yourself in the character's shoes?"

"Actually, David put me in Jody's shoes," I say. "He's the boy in the book."

Ma comes round from the back of the counter and sits on a lumpy stool.

"I was really angry about Pa dying—like Jody was about his pony."

"Yes." She smiles sympathetically.

"Do you think I'm still really angry?"

"Well, from what I just saw upstairs ..." she pauses, making me a little nervous, until she grins, "... I'd say you're on your way to dealing with your anger."

"Don't you wish Pa left us money?"

"Actually, I wish he hadn't left us at all."

"You know what I mean. If he didn't leave us with nothing, less than nothing, then I wouldn't be so angry, would I?" I wouldn't be worrying about hospital bills or rats or my brother's birthday or ways to make money. I'd be a normal kid, maybe going to Belmont Park or to a Royals game or to a social, no invitation required.

She holds onto the broom with both hands and leans her temple against it, like she's holding herself up. "He may not have left us any money, Joey, but he left me with wonderful memories, two wonderful boys, and a wonderful life, better than I could ever have imagined, growing up in Russia."

"If you think everything is so wonderful, why won't you let me drop out of school and run the store full-time?"

"Because you will not be a great businessman with a big company and a huge Westmount mansion on the west side of Park Avenue if you drop out of school to run the store. You've been very clear that you don't want to be like Pa."

Her words sting. My nose and eyes tingle. I stare at the spotless floor. "It's not that I don't ... it's just ... when you say it like that, it sounds bad, Ma. Like I'm bad."

"All children want to do better than their parents, and all parents want their children to do better than them," she says quietly. She leans the broom against the counter and takes my hands in hers. "You're working so hard to take care of David and me, and I'm proud of you. But you know exactly what you want in this life, and you need to go to school for as long as possible to get it, maybe even university. Wouldn't that be wonderful? That's something Pa never got to do. That's the path you must follow."

Yep, those house calls have definitely been about me. What gives Dr. Richter the right to talk about me? But I'm not going to argue about it with Ma. I don't want her having an "episode."

"What if I can't do it?"

"It's better to fail at what you love than to succeed at what you hate. But you won't fail, because you're smart and kind and driven. The real question is, will it all be enough?"

"What do you mean?"

"What happens after we've moved to the west side and we have all the money in the world?"

I think about the last story in *The Red Pony*, about Jody's grandfather and his great big westward adventure with the Indians and the wagon train. And Old Mr. Friedman's great big westward adventure, escaping the Nazis. And Ma's great big westward adventure, moving from Russia to Montreal. All for what? Jody's grandfather has a family who doesn't want him. Old Mr. Friedman doesn't have a family. Ma doesn't have Pa.

"I don't know. All the westward adventure stories I've heard lately don't end very well," I say. I'm afraid that's what will happen to my great big westward adventure to the other side of Park Avenue.

"Then you'll have to change that." She pulls out a wrapped box from under the counter. The card on top says: *Happy 13th Birthday, Joey*. I open it. Inside is Pa's *tallis*, a prayer shawl a boy can wear starting on his bar mitzvah. When he becomes a man. "Just don't ever forget who you are along the way."

Chapter 21

LOSING STREAK

❝Make no mistake. The man can play ball.❞
– Sportswriter Dink Carroll

OCTOBER 1946

"What's the matter with you?"

Ben and I are rushing to Aberdeen School to pick up David. Well, I'm rushing. Ben's limping. Badly. And pretending like it's nothing.

"What do you mean?" he asks.

"You look like you need crutches."

"I'm fine."

"No, you're not. What happened?" I snap. I'm not in a good mood.

"Nothing."

"So you're just limping for fun?"

Ben straightens his leg and walks normally, but he winces and makes this "shhhh" sound through gritted teeth, which tells me it is definitely not nothing. He goes back to limping.

"Going to tell me now?" I ask sarcastically.

"I'll tell you what happened if you tell me why you're acting like the world's coming to an end."

"Fine. You go first."

"I tripped playing basketball. Your turn." That was a lie if I ever heard one.

"The store was robbed last night. We're sleeping one floor up and they take everything from the safe. All that money from Mr. Abelson."

"Oh." He makes that long "shhhh" noise again, then says nothing at all. He limps and winces. I ball my fists and rage.

"Why didn't you put the money in the bank? I told you to put it in the bank weeks ago," Ben says.

"You work for Montreal Capital and Commerce now?"

No answer.

"I was going to pay—" I realize just in time that finishing the sentence with "your father" would not go over well. I had more than enough with all the credits paid up and the extra from my side businesses, but Mr. Wolfe hasn't been around since I got the money. "I was going to pay some bills and I was mad at the bank for not giving me Pa's money, not that there was any. But the safe was locked, Ben. I check it every night and every morning."

"What did the police say?"

"You mean before Ma kicked David and me out of the store to go to school, like it's just any other day? Like this isn't the worst thing to happen to us since Pa died? Like everything I've been working for hasn't just up and vanished?"

"Um … I guess."

"They said whoever took the money knew how to crack a safe."

"Was anything else taken?"

"No."

"Did they leave a trail?"

"Of what—breadcrumbs to find them? No. Even the tin Coca-Cola sign was put right back over the safe."

We reach Aberdeen to find David playing catch with a friend. Although I'm here almost every day, the massive building still gives me the shivers. Normally it looks like a castle, perfect for kings and queens—or the Bernsteins. Today it looks like a prison, perfect for the thief who stole my money.

"Come on, David, we have to go!" I call out. It's freezing and there's snow on the ground. Actual snow. On October 1. I read in the paper that the last time we had snow on October 1 was 1899. Those Louisville players coming in by train tonight are going to have the surprise of their lives.

David turns to me and waves, that loopy grin permanently

stuck on his face the past two weeks. He's so happy to be in school after the polio crisis ... to be a kid again. He skips across the yard and jumps into my arms.

"What was that for?" I ask, forcing a fake loopy grin.

"Look, Joey, I can see my breath!" He blows air out and watches it cloud up. When it disappears, he wraps his arms around Ben's waist, pushing him off-balance. Ben steadies himself, sucks in a whole lot of air to keep from yelping in pain, then pats David on the back.

"Mr. Lerner told everyone I'm the best baseball player in the whole school!" I see Mr. Lerner walking toward us and wonder if David misunderstood.

"Hello, Benjamin. Hello Joseph," he says in a teacherly way—too friendly, too all-knowing. "So nice to see you both."

"You, too, sir," Ben replies.

"Thank you. Joseph, will your mother be coming by one day soon?"

"I don't know. It's easier for me to come straight from school. Why?" I stare at him. Something in his tone sounds like trouble.

"Not a problem. I'll telephone her, then," he says, stepping away.

"You can talk to me."

"Hey, David, let's go play catch." Ben limps away and David skips along by his side.

HEATHER CAMLOT

"It's all right, Joseph. I know how busy you are. David's very proud of your accomplishments." I don't know what accomplishments he's talking about, unless losing my life savings is an accomplishment. I suppose it is. Just not one to be proud of. More like disgusted by.

"I'm not that busy."

He looks me over and I can only imagine that my narrowed eyes, crossed arms, and feet fixed in place—the same henchman stand I took when Danny Drucker didn't want to pay up—tells him he ought to spill.

"David's reading isn't at grade level." Great. Swell.

"It's October. He's only been in Grade 2 for a couple of weeks." Like this is news to him.

"Yes, but he's unable to properly identify, sound out, and write some of the letters of the alphabet. This should have been mastered early last year."

"So he's dumb?" And I was upset about a book report. At least I could read the stupid book.

"No, of course not, Joseph. What does he read at home?"

"The sports page of the newspaper."

"By himself?"

"No. I read it to him."

"He needs to read—and more suitable material—to catch up. Could you ask your mother to take David to the library and read with him, something for his age, picture books, comic books? I'm going to search for the school's copy of *Mike Mulligan and His Steam Shovel*. It was one of your favorites," he says with a smile.

"You remember that?" I'm totally surprised. That was a good book. Not one dead pony.

"I remember lots of things about my students, Joseph. Around the same time, your friend over there saw his first movie, *The Wizard of Oz*, at the community center. He wouldn't talk about anything else for years." He laughs and I have to grin. "I know your family is under tremendous stress, Joseph. I wish I could help right away, but we're short-staffed and overcapacity. As soon as we're able to, we will. I promise you that."

I nod and Mr. Lerner waves to David, who comes running, Ben five steps behind and getting further back.

"Oh, by the way," Mr. Lerner says. "David brought his homemade cardboard baseball diamond to show the class. The kids love it. You may have something there." Huh. Business basic #9: Create a want. Who knew David's driving me nuts could launch a new toy.

Mr. Lerner walks toward the school, while I walk the other way. More of a trot. David is in a half-run and panting to keep up. I slow down to let him and Ben catch up.

"I been practicing my reading, Joey. On nights when

you're in the store, Ma lets me read the sports page to her. I can find Jackie Robinson's name, no problem!"

"I want you to read to me, too," I say, trying to sound calm.

"Can I, really? Now? I'm sure there's lots of 'Jackie Robinson' in the paper today, what with Game 3 yesterday."

"The Royals lost yesterday and Jackie's been playing terrible."

"Big deal. The Royals will still win the series. They gotta win, right, Ben?"

"Right, David."

I roll my eyes. "But they're down two games to one," I say, losing my patience. I'm not in the mood.

"What's the matter with you? Are you forgetting we have Jackie? So he didn't play good in Louisville; you wouldn't either if you had all them mean people booing and calling *you* awful names. He'll show 'em, here at home, where he belongs, with the people who love him. That's what he needs. The Royals will win. You'll see."

Even winded, he can't wipe that smirk off his face. But then, all of Montreal is in the same frenzied state—and this is a hockey town. And this is hockey weather.

"We'll go to the library and get you some real books to read, okay?"

"Fine," he says. How are we going to fix this? We don't have money for a special teacher.

"Where are we going, anyway?" David asks, tossing his baseball into the air and catching it in his well-used glove.

"You have Jewish school and—"

"Ah, applesauce! Don't make me go, Joey. I had enough school for one day."

"Goddamn, David, stop whining and grow up!"

"Joey," Ben utters.

We walk. In silence.

When we arrive, David dejectedly hands over his ball and glove, and we switch book satchels. "See you later," I say, feeling awful.

"Yeah, yeah. Bye, Ben." He trudges between the red-brick posts, across the courtyard, and through the glass doors without one look back.

"I'm gonna go, too." Ben waits for me to say something. When I don't, he starts for home.

"Hey, Ben."

He stops and turns to face me.

"Do you think things will ever get better?"

"What did Mr. Lerner say?"

"David can't read."

"Huh." He leans against a brick post and looks up at the sky. "I think things get better when they can't get any worse."

"What does that mean?"

He shrugs. "A person can only take so much before they have no choice but to fight back."

I'm pretty sure he's not talking about me and David. "There something you wanna tell me?"

"I have some comic books, *Superman, Batman*—stuff like that. I'll bring them over for David."

"Thanks, Ben." I knew he'd avoid the question, but at least I asked.

We go our separate ways, him toward home, me toward synagogue.

Rabbi Gottlieb keeps me the full session. I had no choice but to stay. Ma made it very clear I couldn't come home until it was over. She didn't say I had to pay attention, though, which is good, because I have no idea what Rabbi Gottlieb said. I assume my bar mitzvah is still on. I don't really care.

All I care about is finding the thief who robbed our store last night. I would have had a better chance if Ma had let me talk to the police. What was she thinking, taking over like it's none of my business? Like I can't handle it? Treating me like some kid. Just like Dr. Richter.

The overwhelming smell of garlic hits me as I hit St. Lawrence. Crowds of people are shopping for pickles and bagels and fruit and vegetables and *tchotchkes* and doodads, and everything else you can or can't name. Yelling and screaming and bartering and gossiping all go on in Yiddish. Two men are arguing about something or other, one of them holding up a copy of the Yiddish newspaper *Keneder Adler* in the other man's face. I have no idea what the paper says. I have no idea what the men are saying. But it actually looks like it might come to blows.

I hurry on. As I pass Old Mr. Friedman's flat, I look up. The curtains are wide open. It's cloudy out but I imagine the little bit of light there is beating right down on those *Four Freedoms* posters. I bet tonight Old Mr. Friedman will be sitting in his armchair, facing those posters, with today's *Star* on his lap, grinning from ear to ear as he sucks on his candy and rereads for the umpteenth time the headline that I caught while leaving synagogue: *Goering, Ribbentrop, 10 Other Top Nazis To Be Hanged.* He may not have his family back, but at least their deaths and the millions of others aren't going unpunished.

Unpunished. The thief better not go unpunished. He should be hanged. Hand back our money and then hanged.

"Where are the police?" I ask as soon as I walk in the store.

"They left a while ago." Ma's voice is fake cheery. Her eyes are dark circles from not sleeping again and her skin is pale from the stress of it all.

"And where's our money?"

"They don't know, Joey. They haven't been able to

solve any of the robberies. But they assure me they're doing everything they can."

"Oh, goody. I feel so much better."

"We'll get through this, Joey. It's just money."

"It's just money? Are you—" She cuts me off by taking my face in her shaky hands. She kisses me on the forehead, which is pretty much at her eye level now. Why does she keep acting like everything's okay? Nothing's okay.

"You have a visitor." She pats my cheek, then moves back to the counter and her broom. "Go on. Young men don't leave young ladies waiting."

Chapter 22

CROSSTOWN RIVALRY

❝ *No fan exercises like the baseball fan what he considers the inalienable right to cheer or jeer as he sees fit.* **❞**
— Sportswriter Sam Lacy

I climb the stairs to our flat and find Shelly curled up in Pa's threadbare button-back chair, reading *Nancy Drew: The Mystery of the Tolling Bell*. This is the first time she's ever been up here. The first time she's seen the peeling paint, the lifting kitchen linoleum, the faded area rug, the broken dining chairs, the stained ceiling. All the furniture matches, though. And the place is spotless—Ma wouldn't have it any other way. But I never wanted Shelly to see this. I can't believe Ma let her up here.

"It's not Westmount," I say, grabbing an unbroken chair from the dining table and turning it to face Shelly. But I look down at the rug instead. It doesn't have any emus or ostriches on it, just grape juice stains Ma couldn't completely wash out.

I guess they could pass for exotic birds if you don't stare at them too long.

"I don't live in Westmount," she replies, dog-earring her page.

"It's not Outremont."

Actually, when you stare at the stains, they look more like wild beasts ... with long teeth ... and sharp claws.

"It's your home."

"I'm getting out of here." I glance up to see her smiling. She's always smiling. I have nothing to smile about.

"I know."

Her reddish hair is real shiny today and I can smell her lavender soap. It takes us twenty minutes to heat water for a bath in the flat and, even then, David and I have to use the same water.

"And what if I don't?" I jerk my head back down to stare at my shoes that are so scuffed, no amount of polishing could help.

"What, the great businessman Joseph Grosser, losing his determination?" I know she's still smiling, but I don't look up. "You will. And if not, my pa has plenty."

Did Shelly just ... propose marriage?

Ma won't let me work full-time at thirteen, but Shelly can propose marriage at twelve? I like her and all, but someone's been dipping into her sisters' *Seventeen* magazines. I'm back to staring at Shelly. But not in the way I used to stare at her during bar mitzvah lessons in Rabbi Gottlieb's office. I'm angry. I didn't know I could get angry with Shelly.

"I don't want your father's money. I want my own!"

She straightens up and takes a quick breath.

My voice gets louder with every word. "I want to find the thief who stole all the store's money, sometime between 10 PM last night and 6 AM this morning, so I can beat the stuffing out of him." I could do it, too. I may be small but I'm furious, and that beats size any day.

"Oh, Joey, that's awful! I didn't know. Was it a lot?"

"Yes." I look away. How did I let this happen? I needed that money to pay the hospital bill, to pay Mr. Wolfe. To get out of this dump of a neighborhood. Now it's gone. We have nothing. Less than nothing. We're worse off than when Pa was around. I've completely failed. I can't take care of Ma and David.

"Joey, are you okay? You look really sick."

"Fine," I lie. What am I going to do?

"Let me help you."

"You don't understand, Shelly. It's not just the money." The thought of Mr. Wolfe forcing my hand, making me owe him when I never asked for help, makes me even madder.

"Then explain it to me."

"I can't."

"Can't or won't?"

I shrug, then change the subject. "Why'd you come here? I wish you didn't."

"Why not?"

"This isn't Outremont. It's De Bullion."

"Yes, so you've mentioned. It's your home, Joey. I like it. This is the coziest chair I've ever sat in. It's the perfect reading chair—you can just curl up in it." She snuggles back like she's waiting for the chair to hug her. "The chairs at my house are stiff, and I get yelled at if I put my feet up because I might get the fabric dirty—with my socks." She rolls her eyes. "And I like the books on the shelf over there," she cocks her chin toward the radio. "I had to look through them, Joey, I couldn't help it. I loved *Mike Mulligan and his Steam Shovel* when I was little!"

"We have that?"

"Yes! I could just tell how much you loved it, too. It looks like it's been read a thousand times. And," she smiles, "it's marked Aberdeen School in the front. You must have borrowed it and kept it because you loved it so much."

Guess Mr. Lerner won't be finding the school's copy after all.

"My mom makes us keep all our books in our rooms, and then she goes through them and gets rid of anything she thinks we're too old for. And I love the collection of old photographs hanging on that wall. There must be fifty of them. Some look ancient."

"I don't know who most of those people are." And I don't really care. Ghosts. Dead and gone. They can't help me.

"You should ask."

"It's still not Outremont."

"Oh, so what, Joey? I know you think the other side of Park Avenue is so great, but it's just a place."

"Easy for someone to say who lives there and only comes here once in a while because she has to for her bat mitzvah lessons."

"I came here to see you." Her voice is shaky. She steals a look and turns away, but it's enough time to see her blue-sky eyes fill with tears. "Maybe I should go."

"Yeah, maybe you should."

She stands up, pats the chair pillow to fluff it for whatever reason, picks up her overcoat, and heads to the door.

"I'm sorry," she whispers, facing the door. "I didn't mean to make you more upset. I'm sorry about the robbery."

I don't say anything. She opens the door and runs out.

My legs are numb, my body drained.

What did I do?

I stand there for a minute—which feels like a year—and then race to the door and fly down the stairs as fast as my legs can take me.

HEATHER CAMLOT

"Joey, what happened? Why was Shelly crying?" Ma calls after me as I run through the store. I ignore her and bolt through the front door and down De Bullion Street toward Outremont. I make it to the end of the block, in front of Old Mr. Friedman's place, when I hear his voice.

"What's the matter, kid?"

Mr. Wolfe is standing at the corner. He's decided to show up again.

"Did you see Shelly? Shelly Richter? Argh … did you see a girl run by?" I yell, not caring that he can pummel me into the ground with one giant, bear-like fist.

"Shelly Richter, the doctor's daughter?" he asks. "I knew you hated your father, but I never knew that much."

"What does that mean?" I demand.

"Well, you're dating the daughter of the man who killed him, no?"

"Killed him? He died of a heart attack!"

"Is that what they told you?" He shakes his head. "We gotta talk. Let's go."

Chapter 23

MONEY PITCH

❝ *What Robbie wanted more than anything else was to be treated like any other ball player. But it just didn't work out that way.* **❞**
— Sportswriter Dink Carroll

I'm sitting in the very last seat in the long single line of tables at Schwartz's, opposite Mr. Wolfe. He's ordered us smoked meat sandwiches, *karnatzels*, and cherry colas. I've never been in Schwartz's before and the smoked meat smells almost as good as Ma's *rugelach*. I only wish I had the appetite to eat. I really do. But I'm still thinking about Shelly.

"Kid, you listening to me?" I look up from the straw I've completely gnawed to find Mr. Wolfe staring at me. Great. Swell. He's been going on about something, but I've only heard maybe half of it.

"Why'd you say Shelly's pa killed my pa?"

He takes a big bite of his smoked meat sandwich. His left cheek swells with all the food. He only chews with one side of

HEATHER CAMLOT

his face and his left eye keeps opening and closing. He pushes his top lip out with his tongue, then drags it across his teeth to pull out bits of smoked meat with a sucking sound.

"I've heard stories."

"What kind of stories?"

"Stories unfit for repeating to a kid your age." He gulps down some cherry cola, licks his lips, then rolls up the *karnatzel* in a piece of rye bread covered in mustard.

"But he was my pa's doctor."

"Obviously not a very good one."

"But he saved my ma."

"A lucky shot. Look, kid," he says kindly, "doctors need to make a living just like everyone else."

"Then they probably want alive patients, not dead ones."

He chuckles and takes a mammoth bite of the *karnatzel*. Mustard oozes out the end. "That's a good one, kid. I'm talking about money, payment for services rendered."

"Are you actually saying Pa didn't pay Dr. Richter? So he ... he let him die? Pa saw him at the Herzl; he didn't *have* to pay. And Dr. Richter works at the hospital the other days. He has plenty!" I repeat Shelly's words.

"Everyone can use more."

Let him die ... that's the dumbest thing I've ever heard. It can't be true. Can it? But maybe that's why he's letting Shelly be friends with me. Because he feels bad. No. That's ridiculous. "Doctors don't let people die."

"Unfortunately, doctors do let people die. All the time." He chomps his sandwich, then changes the subject. "How's business?"

"We were robbed." I start gnawing at my straw again.

"That's awful!" The restaurant is crammed with people and the noise level is beyond loud, but at least half the heads still turn to look at us. I look down at the table. "This neighborhood is fulla crooks."

"I was going to pay you back the money for the hospital bill."

"Ah, Joey, I'm real sorry. Was anyone hurt?"

I shake my head and start twisting the straw to pieces.

"Thank God for that. That's most important. You can always make more money." I look up at him.

"I know, I know, easier said than done." He pats my hand. "We're a lot alike, you and me. I also want to be respectable and have lots of money and move out of this hell hole, just like you."

What with all the money Mr. Wolfe seems to have with his gold watch and overpayment for cigarettes and Ben's nice clothes, it's a puzzle why Ben and his family even live in this neighborhood. I don't have a clue.

"I can share some details about that business I was telling you about, though."

Finally.

He looks around the restaurant to make sure no one's listening in.

"I have a meeting with the head of a very big company, a lot of money changing hands. He's a jumpy fellow I'm meeting, trusts no one. You know the type." He rolls his eyes and makes a silly face, poking fun at how scared the guy is. "Some people, right? But then again, with the robbery at the store, no one can be too careful these days. I told him I'd bring an extra set of eyes to stand outside and keep a lookout for anything suspicious. That's all you'd need to do."

"Shouldn't you ask the police, if it's that much money?"

"I can't go to the police with my reputation. I made a lot of bad choices in my life, Joey. The police will never help me."

His face and voice soften, and for a moment, it feels like we're having a private conversation, just him and me in the room, talking, like friends, like family.

"You can go far in this world, Joey. Your father worked like a dog. He was a kind man, a real *mensch*, but not smart like you. You're destined for something better, bigger. But you're stuck, with no real out. This will get you out of your ma's hospital bill, and I'll give you extra to make up for the robbery and invest in all those businesses of yours. All I need is a couple of hours tomorrow afternoon."

I glance up from my straw. Mr. Wolfe's eyes are warm and inviting. "But I have school and I have my bar mitzvah the next morning."

"Yeah, the timing's a little awkward, but we'll meet right after school and you'll be back in plenty of time for your bar mitzvah. If you want to be in the majors, you gotta play like you're in the majors, right?"

I think about what I read in one of those *Sporting News* that David now gets regularly from Old Mr. Friedman. I'm Jackie Robinson, with that burning ambition to prove I can play in the big leagues.

"I do this and I don't owe you anything more?"

"Absolutely. And if we work well together, we'll do it again."

"What about Ben?"

"I'm gonna surprise him when he gets home from school tomorrow. So you gotta keep it secret still."

I nod and raise my hand to shake Mr. Wolfe's, but I accidentally knock over my cola and the bubbly liquid seeps right into his sandwich. Mr. Wolfe's eyes flash cold.

"An accident. It happens," he says, softening again. I return to my mutilated straw. "To the future!" He toasts and chugs the rest of his cherry cola.

Chapter 24

CIRCUS CATCH

❝ *Those prognosticators and baseball fortunetellers*
who predicted Jackie Robinson wouldn't hit
the high brand of pitching in the International League
are running for cover this week. **❞**
— Sportswriter Wendell Smith

October is usually a beautiful month in Montreal. The weather gets cooler, but not so much that you can't be outside, which is good because no one in my neighborhood wants to be inside, especially after we heard about Mrs. Abelson.

The story goes that last week Mrs. Abelson was coming home from a movie with her daughter, Adele, and she was so busy swooning over some actor that she forgot to stomp on the landing before opening the door.

Everyone knows you have to stomp on the landing and swing the door open and closed a couple of times because the vibrations and the wind warn the cockroaches to run and hide. Well, Mrs. Abelson just went ahead and opened the door and turned on the light. Every surface was covered, even weird angles, like along the handle of the kettle and the back of the chesterfield. Adele said it looked like a hostile takeover by a battalion of tiny tanks. Ben says Adele has this thing for talking in war metaphors. I don't know why, but it sure adds lots of drama to a story. While Mrs. Abelson was passed out, Adele went and stomped on the floors to get every last one of those cockroaches to run and hide, like watching a defeated platoon retreat from their occupied territory in the face of their much bigger and much louder enemy. She turned on every last light, hammered on every hard surface, and then pulled her mother onto the chesterfield and gave her a glass of water. I assume she cleaned the glass of cockroach filth first. But I could be mistaken.

We've never had cockroaches the way Ma cleans; at least, I've never seen signs of them, but I've heard they're a lot like rats—slimy, stinky, lightning-fast, eyelash-eating rats.

This week's another story, though. Snow, rain, near-freezing temperatures. Spectators will be shivering in the stands at Delorimier Stadium tonight, that's for sure, but they'll be happy to be outside if it means watching Game 4 of the series. Just like the folks in my neighborhood will still be happy to be outside if it means avoiding the cockroaches.

A block away from St. Lawrence, I can already smell the fresh-from-the-oven bagels, the swirl of honey, malt, and smoke. I can hear the fruit man calling out to passersby to buy apples. There's also a low hum that gets louder with every step. As I round onto the Main, which is what we call St. Lawrence for some reason, that hum booms with all the people chatting, laughing, bargaining, peddling. Enjoying.

"Hiya, Joey," says Mr. Tarasofsky, a chain of at least fifty house keys around his neck so he can deliver his bottles of milk right to people's iceboxes.

"Hi, Mr. Tarasofsky. You're working pretty far south today," I call back and he nods, the keys jingling together.

"We picked a nice day for a walk, didn't we, Joey?" Mr. Brownstein jokes as we meet on the street.

"Yes, sir. Business good?" He nods and we keep moving.

"Joey, it's been a long time." Mr. Kis. I haven't seen him since the day I ran into his pharmacy to get Aspirin for Pa. I shift uneasily, but his bright eyes and warm smile make me smile right back.

"Hello, Mr. Kis—yeah, I guess so. Late lunch?" I ask, looking at his brown paper bag that, by the smell, is most definitely a Schwartz's smoked meat sandwich.

Mr. Kis laughs and holds up his bag. "Yes, but don't tell Mrs. Kis. She'll kill me and then tell me I'm ruining my appetite for dinner!"

"My lips are sealed. You know, we're making sandwiches at the store, too. You should stop by sometime." Business basic #10: Promote, promote, promote.

"You're quite the businessman, Joey. I'll do just that, thank you."

"I gotta run." Mr. Wolfe will kill me if I'm even a minute late meeting him. I should've found a quieter route to take. I hope no one tells Ma they saw me. Too late to think about that now.

I cross St. Lawrence and see Mr. Wolfe do a little dance next to a fancy new car. Long hood, short trunk, white-wall tires, so sharp. It looks like a car Frank Sinatra would drive. I'll have to ask Ben about that. I'm sure one of his *Movie Life* magazines must have had Sinatra standing next to a car.

"Wow! Where'd you get it?"

"I bought it," he says quickly.

"Did you rob a bank?" I ask, forgetting for a second that Mr. Wolfe does not have a sense of humor.

"Why don't you hop inside? It's even better." He opens the door and I breathe in that new-leather smell. Reminds me of the baseball glove Ben gave David for his birthday. I climb in to luxury.

Ben's crouched in the back with his black oxfords on the tan seat and his arms wrapped around his legs. His cap's sitting real low on his forehead, making dark shadows on his eyes. At least they look like dark shadows.

"Hey, you're here!" I say, excited.

HEATHER CAMLOT

"What are *you* doing here?" he says, angry.

I feel a weight drop in my stomach. Mr. Wolfe never told him. All Ben knows is that I made him a promise to stay away from his pa. A promise I've broken a dozen times.

"Get out of the car!" Ben yells.

"Benjamin Wolfe, you don't treat your best friend like that," Mr. Wolfe orders as he slides into the driver's seat. "He's here doing me a favor. Ease up."

"You said if I came, Joey wouldn't have to," he yells at Mr. Wolfe. "Why is he here?"

"The more the merrier," Mr. Wolfe says as he starts the car.

"He doesn't need you, Joey! Go home! Go home now!" His eyes are threatening me, just like the night we almost got killed by the streetcar on the way to the party in Westmount. I feel sick. Half of me is in the car, wanting the opportunity, needing the money Mr. Wolfe promised me. The other half is still outside the car, wanting to run like Ben's telling me.

Whatever I choose, I lose. I lose Ben.

At the loud blast of a car horn, Ben breaks eye contact and snaps his head toward the street-side window.

"Joey, look ..." I follow Ben's pointing index finger. I look out at the other side of the street. My stomach, already queasy, churns.

"David?"

"He ain't invited, Joey," Mr. Wolfe says, irritated, looking over from the front seat.

"I know, I know." I jump out of the car. Mr. Wolfe slides out after me and slams his door. I head toward the intersection to cross St. Lawrence. I'd dropped David off at the store with Ma after school. What is he doing here?

"Get back in the car, Joey," Mr. Wolfe calls out to me, then drops a bear-like paw on my shoulder as I stop dead at the edge of the Main, waiting for a break in the stream of cars heading north and the lineup heading south. St. Lawrence is a mess. They should really make it one way.

I glance at the paw. My stomach churns faster. "David, what are you doing here? You have to go home!" I shout at the top of my lungs, hoping he can hear me.

David blindly takes a step closer. His eyes are focused on me, not at the cars rocketing by.

"NO!" I shout, my heart racing. "Stay there!"

"The kid can go home on his own, Joey. Get in the car." Mr. Wolfe's hot breath prickles the back of my neck. His hand slides from my shoulder down my arm and he wraps his beefy fingers around it. But he doesn't yank or pull. He squeezes. Hard.

"I know he can go home on his own, but he's trying to cross the street!" I yell.

"You owe me money, Joey. This is the repayment. Get in."

I turn away to see David looking petrified, but still trying to cross. "Don't cross!"

"Joey." Mr. Wolfe's red eyes grab mine. They penetrate so deep I can't look away, and I feel myself walking toward the car like I'm under some sort of spell.

"That's it, kid." He smiles, flashing the same sharp yellow teeth as the pit bull. "I gotta brief you on what we're doing before we reach our destination. We don't want anything to go wrong. I'm about to take you to the west side of Park Avenue."

Ben jumps out of the car and stomps on Mr. Wolfe's foot. Hard. Real hard. A manic grin creeps onto Mr. Wolfe's face. He lets go of my arm and smacks Ben across the cheek. Hard. Real hard.

"Run, Joey!" Ben yells as he hits the cement.

I stare at Ben in complete shock. His black eyes so obvious now. Two black eyes. My mouth is wide open but I can't speak.

"Get David!" he yells again.

I back away quickly, then spin around to see David step on the road, with traffic swift and furious. Another loud and long honk and I bolt for the other side of the Main, clambering around the oncoming traffic, banging onto the front hood of a black roadster with a young couple inside looking on in horror, rolling off, scrambling back to my feet, running, running, heart pounding like it's never pounded before, even with being chased by that pit bull, hearing but not listening to warnings that I'm going to get myself killed, reaching the other side, the east side, scooping David up in my arms, and falling in a heap on the sidewalk.

"What ... were you thinking ... following me?" I can't catch my breath. Clutching David against my chest makes it even harder to take in any air. I take the deepest breath I can—twenty balloons full—to quell the sick feeling.

"I ... I wasn't thinking ..." He raises his red face to mine.

"No, you weren't thinking at all. You could've been killed!" All the screeching, all the honking, all the yelling still swirl in my head.

"I ... I'm ... I ..." David lays his wet face on my shoulder. His breath is hot as he whimpers. He sniffles back tears that he doesn't want to let fall, for all the good it's doing. I wrap my arms around him tightly.

"It's okay, David. I'm here. You're safe."

A woman in a belted trench coat and royal blue scarf (it looks like one of Mrs. Abelson's) reaches down and hands us each a tissue, while the man she's with, also wearing a royal blue scarf, asks if there's anything they can do. I look up at them, and then across the street for Mr. Wolfe's car. I can't see Ben or Mr. Wolfe. But I can hear tires screech against the pavement as a car peels out and speeds away. I should be with Ben. Two black eyes. The smack across the cheek. I'm not the one who needs help. I shake my head at the couple and they rush off. I look back at David.

"Why'd you leave the store?" I ask. The fog lifts, the pounding slows. Mr. Wolfe is gone.

"Pa told me to," he replies weakly.

"You mean Ma. She knows I'm not home?"

"No, I mean Pa."

I feel under his mop of hair for some sort of bump where he must have hit his head against the sidewalk when I came barrelling across. I can't find any and he doesn't scream in pain when I push into his skull. I look into his eyes, not actually knowing what I'm supposed to be looking for, but they're just red from crying.

"Pa's dead."

"I know."

"Does he talk to you a lot?" Can a seven-year-old go crazy?

"Can we go home now?" he asks, ignoring my question. It's just as well. I don't think I want to know the answer, anyway.

I push myself to standing, then pull him to his feet. We walk the four blocks back to the flat.

"Pa thinks you're doing a good job," David finally says when we reach the store's door. "But he thinks you should play ball with me more."

Chapter 25

VISITING TEAM

❝He had become part of our team the day we began throwing at those who threw at him.❞
– Jean-Pierre Roy, Montreal Royals pitcher

Pa thinks I'm doing a good job, according to David. A good job at what—losing all our money, almost getting my brother killed, watching my best friend get beat up by his pa?

I drop David off at the store and tell him to stay put. He doesn't need to be told twice. He grabs his baseball from the counter and disappears into his hiding spot. I hear the thump ... thump ... thump of the ball against the wall.

"Joey, what's going on?" Ma asks.

"I need Ben's address," I demand. That's not going to go over well.

"Excuse me?"

"Ma, please. I know about the deal between Pa and Mrs. Wolfe. I get it. But I need to find Ben. Right now."

She looks me over, then writes the address on the front page of the newspaper, tears it off, and hands it to me.

"Go."

She could have said no. She could have asked a million questions. She didn't do either. She trusts me. So why don't I trust myself?

Because I can't keep a promise.

And now there's another promise I have to break. The one made between Pa and Mrs. Wolfe.

I head to Ben's house.

As I walk west toward Clark Street, I wonder what Ben and Mr. Wolfe are doing right now. I wish I'd gone with them. Not because of the money I owe, but because of Ben. I should have stayed. I should have stayed with him, not run. Those two black eyes hidden in the shadow of his cap. That slap in the face. But I couldn't stay with Ben and save David at the same time, could I?

I cross Mount Royal Avenue and start looking at the house numbers. Midway down the block I find it. A gray stone triplex with the typical winding staircase. I climb the stairs to the second floor and knock. The curtain in the door window moves, barely. I can see a sliver of a face—one eye, one cheek, one corner of a mouth. That eye is open real wide, like it's surprised, or scared.

"Joey. Well, I certainly wasn't expecting you," Mrs. Wolfe says with a shaky voice as she opens the door just enough to poke her face through. I never realized Ben was the spitting image of his ma, although seeing as he doesn't look anything like Mr. Wolfe, I guess that makes sense. Green eyes, wavy brown hair, Frank Sinatra smile. Looking at Mrs. Wolfe makes me feel even worse for leaving Ben.

"Does your mother know you're here, dear?" She drums her fingers on the inside of the door, like she doesn't have time for my visit. I wonder what she and Pa planned if I ever showed up.

"Yes."

"I see. Well, even so, I'll tell Ben you're looking for him." She quickly moves to close the door.

But I hold it open. "Mrs. Wolfe, is Ben home?"

"No, dear. He went off with his father right after school."

"Do you know where?"

"No, Joey, I'm afraid I don't. I'm sorry, but I really must ask you to leave." She looks past me to see if anyone is watching. Like this is some kind of test.

"I know all about the deal you made with Pa, Mrs. Wolfe. I wouldn't be here if it wasn't important."

"Then you also know it's best you run home." She closes the door. I hear the sharp scrape of a lock.

I clank down the stairs, feeling the metal reverberate in my feet, like mild electric shock. I have no idea where to find Ben or Mr. Wolfe, and I'm not ready to go home. For what? When I hit Mount Royal Avenue, I take a hard right and head into Outremont.

It's been one whole day since I've seen Shelly. I don't know what to do or say, so I stand at the far end of the island in the road across from her house. Thinking. Waiting. A black car pulls into the driveway and Dr. Richter climbs out, holding his medical bag in one hand and a massive bouquet of flowers in the other. Funny that he buys them when he could just pick some from his garden. He taps the front door with his foot. Shelly opens the door. I panic and spin around so she can't see me—like a kid who plays peekaboo and thinks he's hiding because his hands are over his own eyes. It seems like forever before I hear the door close again, and when it finally does, I turn back to face Shelly's house.

And Shelly.

"What are you doing here?" Her stare slices into me from two feet away.

"Um ..." I'm sweating something awful as she buttons up her sweater.

"I've never done anything mean to you."

I shake my head to agree.

"And I think I've been a pretty good friend."

Now I nod to agree.

"Then why? I like you, Joey, and you made me cry." She starts to tear up again, and I want to punch myself for making her.

"I came to talk," I say real low.

"So talk." She crosses her arms and waits.

"I'm sorry."

"For what?"

She's going to make me say it. Guess that's fair.

"I'm sorry for being mean and making you cry. I just ... I was really mad and ... you were there, so I took it out on you. I shouldn't have. I didn't mean to. I'm sorry."

"Shelly, you have to come in for dinner!" her sister calls from the doorstep.

Shelly turns and runs back across the road. I follow her.

"Will you come for lunch tomorrow after our b'nai mitzvah?" I ask from the sidewalk.

"I thought you didn't want me at your house," she says from her front step.

"I do."

"I'll think about it."

I think she smiles before closing the door. I could be mistaken. I really hope I'm not.

Chapter 26

JELLY LEGS

❝ *Jack Robinson is a fine type of young man, intelligent and college-bred, and I think he can take it too.* **❞**
– Branch Rickey, president and general manager of the Brooklyn Dodgers

I glance over at the clock. Five-thirty AM. I've been lying in bed all night, thinking about Ben and Mr. Wolfe. What did they do? Where did they go? Is Ben all right?

I get up, walk around, gulp a glass of water, lie down, get up because I have to go to the bathroom, lie down, think about what's the matter with me. Think about why I always hurt the people who are good to me. Ben. Shelly.

I think about Shelly and how I was such a jerk; think about Dr. Richter and how he must think I'm such a jerk; think about Rabbi Gottlieb and how he must think I'm such a jerk, too, because even though he's a rabbi and is supposed to be forgiving and all, he's still Shelly's grandfather and family comes first, and even here in my bed, he's still staring at me, and it's because he thinks I'm going to mess up my bar mitzvah, which is only in another few hours; and then I start thinking about what's going to happen in another few hours—namely messing up my bar mitzvah—and that keeps me awake even more.

An hour of lessons every week, then an hour of lessons twice a week for an entire year. I could've been making money to get out of this rat-infested flat. And as if on cue, that rat in the rafters shows up. I can hear it scurrying, its sharp little claws making quick clicking sounds, faster than the ticking of a clock. Great. Swell.

I stand up and shuffle over to David, who's sleeping like he doesn't have a care in the world. I check his ears. They're still there. No rats gnawing on them. I move back to my bed, but I don't bother lying down.

I gotta see Ben.

I slip on some clothes and a pair of sneakers, and quietly cross the living room, trying not to bang into anything, but since we don't have that much furniture, it's pretty easy. Those faded family photographs follow me as I walk. The way the sliver of light from the window hits the wall makes all those faces look alive. With a shiver, I reach the front door. Soon I'm on De Bullion Street. The air is much warmer than the past few days and the sky is clear. I begin reciting my bar mitzvah so when Rabbi Gottlieb stares at me, it will be because I amazed him and not because I messed up.

You know how you know a place so well that you can walk it without thinking about where you're going? I don't even remember turning onto Park Avenue, but here I am, right in front of the angel statue. I look up at the mountain. The rising sun tears along Rachel Street, through Fletcher's Field, and straight for Mount Royal, all that light making the leaves of the red oaks and sugar maples burst with the brightest reds and oranges and golds. It's like a painting. A breeze blows and the leaves sway. I breathe in their smoky, earthy smell. Mount Royal at dawn is the most beautiful thing I've ever seen.

As the Number 29 streetcar rumbles by and sets off a trackful of caps, the mountain smell is replaced with charcoal, saltpeter, and sulfur. The dancing leaves slow and stop.

"Joey!" Old Mr. Friedman is across the street, calling me over. I wave back and set my course for his newspaper stand, the front stacked high with the latest editions, the back lined with glossy magazines, and the awning draped with unfolded front pages. As I get closer, I walk faster and rub my eyes, like it'll change what I'm seeing.

BANK ROBBERY GONE WRONG! the headline screams. I get a real bad feeling in my gut. My feet can't move quick enough. My eyes sting, I don't know why, but I can see clearly enough to read trouble all over Old Mr. Friedman's face. I grab the newspaper he holds out for me and try to focus, try to read. Every word.

One dead, one injured in shoot-out, it says under the headline. My throat tightens.

"Big news this morning," Old Mr. Friedman starts uneasily. "Your friend?"

I gaze up at him and he meets my stinging eyes. I know why they're stinging.

I continue reading:

An armed man broke into the new Westmount branch of the Montreal Capital and Commerce Bank on Wednesday after closing, only to find security guard Mr. Max Abelson and bank manager Mr. Richard Buck still in the building. According to an officer who arrived on the scene, the man threatened to kill Mr. Buck if he didn't hand over the money he was preparing for the vault. In response to Mr. Abelson's plea to disarm, the man turned his gun on the security guard.

Mr. Abelson, a World War I veteran, drew his sidearm quickly. The man fired at Mr. Abelson and struck him in the leg. Not a moment later, a teenage boy ran into the bank, straight to the downed guard, and picked up the sidearm.

Mr. Buck later explained that Mr. Abelson recognized the boy and begged him to drop the weapon. He refused and pointed it at the armed man, who then yelled, "What the hell are you doing? Get the money and get out of here!"

The boy replied: "I won't let you kill him!" The man aimed his gun at the boy, but was felled by a bullet in the back from Mr. Buck.

The man is Mr. Uzzi Wolfe, 38.

Mr. Abelson was taken to hospital for treatment of injuries, and the boy for shock. Mr. Wolfe was pronounced dead on arrival.

"I'm sorry," Old Mr. Friedman says, his voice cracking.

I nod and swallow hard. I reach into my pockets to get some money. I don't have a cent on me. I'm frozen in place.

"Joey, take the paper."

"No, I can't."

"It's your bar mitzvah day. You're a man now and all men must read the newspaper. Whatever news it delivers. Take it."

"No, I—"

"*Oy, boychik.* You don't let anyone do anything for you. Fine. I'll write it down as a credit. Pay me later. Or I can make it your bar mitzvah gift."

"Thank you."

He shakes his head, like he's disappointed by my answer. "All you can do right now is go home and get dressed for your bar mitzvah."

"But I can't. This … this …" I can't even say the words. I just shake the paper in his face.

"There are good people and bad people in this world, brave people and cowardly. You must be brave." He watches me, the way Pa used to watch me when he would teach me something new about the store and see how fast I could figure it out on my own. I need to see Ben. But I already know the hospital won't let me in.

I run all the way home, my head trying to digest what I read. I scale the stairs two at a time, shove the door open, and get hit by the smell of salami and eggs frying in oil.

"Where have you been?" Ma comes running from the kitchen, her apron covering her new outfit, a sharp dress suit the color of wine. Her hair is up, not one strand out of place, and she has makeup on. She looks so nice. She pats down my hair, wipes beads of sweat from my face with her apron, and stares at me hard. "What's the matter?"

I unroll the newspaper and raise it to her face.

She gasps, cups a hand over her mouth, and clutches the back of Pa's old armchair to catch herself. Her eyes dart from side to side as she reads the article, then she locks eyes with me, staring at me over the headline. She takes a deep breath, straightens herself, and holds my face in her hands.

"I can't do this. I can't go through with my bar mitzvah. Not without Ben. Not with what's happened."

She leans her forehead against mine. "Ben would be the first person to tell you to go. He's the best friend I could have hoped for you."

"I don't think he cares about me much anymore. I was rotten to him. I should have been there."

"Should have been where?" Her hands are now damp and tight on my cheeks.

"I mean, I just ... I should have been there for him, been a better friend."

She lowers her hands. "You'll work out whatever happened between you. Go call the hospital and find out how Ben is. I'll be right back." I can hear her turn off the gas and scrape what is probably very dry salami and eggs out of the frying pan and onto a plate, with a small *thwack* at David's hand to keep him away from my breakfast.

The telephone operator puts me through to a hospital. I hope it's the right one. Ma's back by my side.

"Montreal General Hospital. How may I help you?" the nasally voice on the other end says.

"Benjamin Wolfe, please. My name is Joseph Grosser."

I don't know what I'm supposed to say. Is that what I'm supposed to say?

"One moment, please."

I pace back and forth the short distance of the telephone cord, sweat beading all over again, and I wait for what feels like a lifetime.

"Joey?" I freeze at the sound of a woman's voice.

"Yes?"

"Hello, dear, it's Mrs. Wolfe."

"How's Ben? Is he okay? Can I speak to him?" I blurt out.

"The doctor says Ben is stable, which means he's just fine." I mouth the words *he's okay* to Ma. "He's sleeping right now, but I'll certainly tell him you called. That will make him very happy."

"Can I come to the hospital? When can I see him?"

"The doctor assures me he'll be allowed to go home late this afternoon. You can see him then. I don't want you to worry, all right?"

"Yes, ma'am."

"Thank you for calling, Joey. You're a dear friend." The phone goes dead.

I walk to my bedroom, the newspaper still in my hand. I go through the motions of changing into my suit. In the bathroom, I look in the mirror as I brush my teeth and then my hair. I don't look or feel anything like a man. I feel like a kid who doesn't know which way is up or down, right or left, right or wrong, good or bad.

I feel like a kid who's coming undone.

That's why Mr. Wolfe fixed it so Mr. Abelson got the job at the bank. So he could walk right in and steal from someone who owed him. Did he really think Mr. Abelson would just turn a blind eye to a bank robbery? He did.

That's why Mr. Wolfe paid Ma's hospital bill. So I'd walk right in with him because he made it so I owed him. Did he really think I would rob a bank with him? He did.

He bet on me and Mr. Abelson. And he lost.

His life.

Ben could have lost his life, too.

"Joey—we have to go," Ma calls from the living room.

I pitch the newspaper as hard as I can against the bedroom wall and watch it slip down to the floor and land on David's busted shoes. Before Branch Rickey signed Jackie Robinson to the Royals, he asked him if he had the guts to play ball no matter what.

Do I have the guts to be a man?

I open the linen closet and dig through the cream, Aspirin, and slabs of soap to get to the Old Spice bottle. I lift the stopper and dab on Pa's cologne.

"Let's get this bar mitzvah over with," I say to Ma as I head toward the door. Her head jolts up as I pass, and I could swear time stops for a second.

"What's that smell?" David asks with his nose all crinkled up as he and Ma join me at the door. She's staring at me. The corners of her mouth curl up. I know what she wants to say, and I kind of want to hear it.

"That's the smell of strength. With a hint of forgiveness."

Chapter 27

CALLED UP

❝Robinson seems to have the same sense of the dramatic that characterized such great athletes as Babe Ruth, Red Grange, Jack Dempsey, Bobby Jones, and others of that stamp. The bigger the occasion, the more they rise to it. ❞
– Sportswriter Dink Carroll

Standing on the *bima*, the stage in the synagogue, is terrifying. Like how Jackie Robinson must have felt stepping onto the field for his first Royals game ever. Like how Ben must have felt stepping into the bank. Okay, this isn't that bad, but that kind of moment when you think, *How in the world did I get myself into this?*

I look around at all the people watching me. Ma is sitting in the first row on the women's side, next to Mrs. Richter and Shelly's sisters, all red hair, blue eyes, dressed to the nines. Behind them, Shelly's friends.

On the men's side, David sits front and center, sandwiched between Dr. Richter in a smart-looking suit and Old Mr. Friedman, his work clothes dressed up with a coat and tie. One row back, the stunned looks on my friends' faces tell me they've all seen the newspaper. They probably read the headline as they walked to synagogue this morning. Ben may not have been named, but it's obvious to anyone who knows him. Everyone loves Ben. I imagine him in the store, quiet and safe.

Safe. Away from Mr. Wolfe. The bear of a man Ben warned me about. Who Pa protected me from. Ben told David his pa was already dead. He told me I was better off without a father than having anything to do with his. But I didn't listen. Armed robbery was Mr. Wolfe's new business venture. He knew all along I wouldn't want to have anything to do with it if I knew what it actually was, so he tried to force me into it. He forced Ben, too. Now Mr. Wolfe's dead. A horrible death, just like Mrs. Abelson wished on him. I could have been dead, too. If it weren't for David.

If it weren't for Pa.

Is Pa really talking to David? Has he been trying to talk to me?

My fists ball up and I take a very deep, wheezy breath. I quickly look away from the audience and onto the *bima*.

Shelly. She stands right across from me, on the other side of the reading desk. Her hair hangs down her back, two pieces falling forward to frame her rosy face. She looks pretty in her turquoise dress, but the color is dull compared to her eyes.

HEATHER CAMLOT

"Ahem."

I break away from staring at Shelly to see Rabbi Gottlieb staring at me. I smile a little, then pull on Pa's prayer shawl and kiss the tassels. It smells of Old Spice. I return to Shelly, who urges me on without saying a word. She doesn't seem mad at me anymore. Maybe she also saw the paper.

My mind is swimming with what needs to be done, what has to be said, what's already happened, so that I'm blind to all the movement I'm sure is going on around me. I hear the audience stand up in the presence of the Torah, the first part of the Hebrew bible, that I seem to be holding. I hear Old Mr. Friedman cough and I'm sure he's popping a Life Saver. I hear Ma sniffling—happy about my bar mitzvah, sad that Pa's not here to witness it. I carry the Torah scroll to the reading desk and Rabbi Gottlieb unrolls it.

I glance at Shelly again. She's looking as anxious as I am. We silently give each other the go ahead, and I raise a tassel to the Torah scroll, kiss it, and do my recitation. I don't think I stumbled. I could be mistaken. At least Rabbi Gottlieb isn't staring at me. His full attention is on his granddaughter, who's reading her portion from a slip of paper because of some strange religious rule I don't really get.

When Shelly and I finish, we say more prayers. I return the Torah to its place in the ark and Rabbi Gottlieb says a few words—what exactly, I have no idea. Everyone in the audience stands up. The ceremony's over. Rabbi Gottlieb nudges me off the *bima* and toward the small crowd that wants to congratulate me with *mazel tovs* and handshakes and pats on the back.

I walk.

Right past the well-wishers. Right out of the synagogue. Right up to Park Avenue. Right up to the angel statue. Right up to the red and orange and gold maples and oaks on Mount Royal.

Right up to the Regent Theatre. Right up to Adele Abelson, who was supposed to get us into the Bernstein party but, as the butler said, "was unable to attend due to a work commitment." Was this her work commitment? She's washing the windows. I don't know what I'm doing here.

Yes, I do. Ben loves the movies.

"We're not open yet," she says, concentrating on a speck of dirt that won't come off, no matter how hard she scrubs. I know how she feels. She glances over without lowering her hand. Her green eyes are red and her freckled face is streaked with tears.

"You're Ben's friend," she says, looking me over.

"Yeah," I say, my feet getting set to run. "How ... how's your father?"

"He's still at the hospital, but Ma says he's going to be okay. Hospital wouldn't let me see him. I thought they at least let in family. Couldn't see Ben, either. But he's also going to be okay. My ma saw him."

I nod and my mouth opens to speak. It shuts without a word.

She lowers her arm and tosses the rag into a bucket. "Come on," she says, unlocking the door and waving me in. "It's not really Ben's thing, but it'll do you some good."

Ben's thing. How does she know Ben's thing? Unless this is how he sees all the movies. Through Adele. Or maybe with Adele. I didn't know they were friends. Good friends, it seems. How did I not know? Why didn't Ben tell me? What else hasn't he told me? Based on the last twenty-four hours, I'm guessing a whole heck of a lot.

My eyes tear up as I follow Adele. As often as I see her parents at our store, I've never seen her come in. I've never even seen her at school. I wonder if she dropped out to work when Mr. Abelson lost his job. Lots of kids have.

She smiles protectively and shows me to a seat right by the exit—"Ben's seat," she whispers—then disappears. A minute later, a light flickers from the projection booth. The title *Little Giant* appears on the screen. Abbott and Costello. A comedy.

I cry for the first time in my so-called adult life.

Chapter 28

EXPANDED ROSTER

*❝He was pummelled, besieged and the Royal room
was filled with well wishers. ❞*
– Sportswriter Lloyd McGowan

Still bleary-eyed after the movie, I roam along Park Avenue,
back to the angel statue, and stand in the exact same spot I did
early this morning when I watched the leaves. There's no breeze
blowing anymore and the leaves look lifeless. Ready to fall.

I walk through Fletcher's Field and down to De Bullion.
Every step feels like an incredible effort and just when it seems
like I'll never get any closer, I realize I'm here, standing in front
of the store. I'm home. With tired legs and tired heart, I make
my way up the stairs. I take a deep breath and open the door.

The picture I had of what would come next is completely
opposite to what I see. Crowded into the tiny flat and around
the dining table draped with the whitest tablecloth I've ever
seen, and set with the finest china I never knew we owned,

HEATHER CAMLOT

are my family and friends. David is *schmearing* way too much cream cheese on a bagel, his plate already filled with vegetables, which I'm sure he didn't put there. Dr. Richter is doubled up over something Old Mr. Friedman must've just said, himself unwrapping a candy to stop the cough he caused by his own laugh. Shelly—she's here—is settled with her latest copy of Nancy Drew by her side. And Ma, in her splattered apron over her fine *shul* clothes, is carrying a silver—really, silver!—tray of lox. It reminds me of Norman Rockwell's *Freedom from Want*.

I clear my throat just enough to let them know I'm here. Everyone looks up.

"I …" I don't know what to say. Ma quickly puts the tray down at the head of the table, rushes toward me, cups her hands on my face, and kisses my forehead.

"Mrs. Wolfe called," she whispers. "She said Ben's sorry he couldn't make it to the bar mitzvah."

I choke on how ridiculous that sounds, how very Ben that sounds.

"But he expects you at his house at 4 PM." His house.

"I'm sorry for leaving *shul*." I look down at her wrists, but she stoops her shoulders and tilts her head to make eye contact.

"It's a very emotional day for all of us." She waits a second for me to agree with her. "You performed the bar mitzvah beautifully, and the timing of your exit does not undo what you've accomplished today. Now," she smiles, "come eat. Before your brother finishes everything."

I smile. She gasps and brings her fingers to her lips, kind of like she did this morning when I told her about Ben.

"What's the matter?" I ask, completely unsure what I could have done by ... by what ... smiling?

She lowers her hand and looks straight into my eyes. "It's back," she says softly.

"What's back?"

"The twinkle in your eye. I haven't seen it since ..." Her eyes get glassy and her cheeks flush. She takes a deep breath, closes her eyes to stop herself from crying, then takes my hand and leads me to the head of the table, where I take my place as the man of the house. I look around. Everyone is watching me—David with his loopy grin, Ma with her ready-to-take-on-the-world smile, Old Mr. Friedman with his candy (definitely lemon), Dr. Richter with his fatherly pride, and Shelly—Shelly who should hate me. She smiles shyly and I smile shyly back. Which makes us both smile even more.

"*Nu?*" Old Mr. Friedman says as he lifts his glass of wine. Everyone follows, then waits. I raise my glass and say the prayer over the wine.

The room is quiet, like they're waiting for me to say something else. What do you say on a day like today? When a worst fear comes true and a high honor is given at the same time? Where you're surrounded by all the people who love you and who you love. Minus two. I say the only thing that comes to mind: "*L'chaim.*" To life.

"*L'chaim*!" they repeat, and we drink.

"Grape juice?" Shelly and I cry out together. So much for becoming adults.

Chapter 29

GRAND SLAM

*I'd want [my son] to combine the wisdom of Joe Louis
with the courage of Jackie Robinson. I'd hope for him
to have Jackie's ability to hold his head high in adversity,
the willingness to withstand the butts and digs
and meanness of those who envy him.*
— Sportswriter Sam Lacy

I sit in Pa's threadbare button-back chair with a butter knife
to slice open the envelopes guests gave Ma after the bar
mitzvah. Each one is filled with a little bit of money. A good
start at replacing our savings. The savings Mr. Wolfe stole to
pay his own debts. Seems he was very good at taking bets,
but not very good at making them. He spent what he had
and what he didn't have. On fancy gold watches. On fancy
cars. That's why Ben lives on the east side of Park Avenue,
even with all the money Mr. Wolfe seemingly made in the
gambling business. There was never enough to move to the
west side.

"*Boychik*, I gotta get back to the newsstand. But I want
you to open my gift." Old Mr. Friedman sits down on a dining

chair and hands me a flat package wrapped in newspaper. Ma stands just beside me to watch.

I carefully unwrap the gift. On top is a book by Dale Carnegie called *How to Win Friends & Influence People.*

"I've heard about this book before," I say, flipping through it.

"Sure, why not? It's a business book, after all. But I think you'll find the methods a little less aggressive than your own and much more effective. At the very least, no one will want to wring your neck."

Ma laughs. She actually laughs. I haven't heard Ma laugh in a long time. Old Mr. Friedman watches her with a great big smile on his face. I think he's missed that sound, too, because he slaps his knee and hoots hard. The result: a hacking cough, then a candy popped into his mouth.

"I'll study it hard," I say.

"*Gut.* Now, open the other gift."

I remove the paper around the other flat gift and let out ten balloons worth of air. It's a painting. And it's signed. *A. Friedman.*

"I painted it last week."

"I thought you quit." I follow the swirl of leaves in bright shades of red, orange, and gold, like the leaves on Mount Royal, rising up to heaven.

"Ech ... once an artist, always an artist. I was inspired.

Maybe you can hang it in your Westmount home with all your Chagalls one day."

"I'll hang it today. Our walls can do with some real art from a real artist. It's amazing."

"Why?" He wants a good answer, just like he did that day in his flat. And I've got one for him.

"Because it makes me happy and sad at the same time, it makes me think of Pa—maybe the leaves are going to see him and remind him of us."

Old Mr. Friedman stares at me. A tear gathers in his left eye and rolls down his cheek. He stands up and pats my head.

"That's *gut*, *boychik*," he says slowly, quietly. "Very *gut*." He hugs Ma, looks back at me as he reaches the door, shakes his head with a smile, and heads out. I watch Ma go into the kitchen.

"Here's one more."

I turn to find Dr. Richter taking over Old Mr. Friedman's chair, one of the posts popping out. I smile, embarrassed, and quickly set it back in for him.

He hands me a thin envelope.

"I don't want your money, sir." I try to say it politely, but I don't think I was successful. I could be mistaken.

"Oh, yes, I'm well aware," he says with a grin. I gaze over at Shelly, who's reading torn-out baseball news to David. Our parents arranged it so that we'd have our parties at different times. Ma preferred a small brunch on the day of the bar mitzvah, while Mrs. Richter wanted to throw a huge party on Sunday. It all worked out well, even though I didn't think, after everything that's happened, that any of the Richters would come to my house ever again. Or that I'd still be invited to Shelly's.

"There's no money in the envelope," Dr. Richter says. I put it on the pile on my lap.

"Thank you," I say. I struggle to make eye contact with Dr. Richter. I want to ask him a question, need to ask him a question, but when I do finally look at him, I feel childish. Like getting the answer will change everything and I'll have to grow up.

"What's bothering you?" he asks.

Here goes.

"Ben's father told me you killed Pa." I know that's not going to go over well. It sounds so awful. I immediately look down at the envelopes in my lap.

"I see," he whispers. "And what do you think?" His hushed voice actually scares me. He's gotta be angry. But it's not Mr. Wolfe angry. It's not even Ben angry. It's—I don't know—shock? Hurt? I can feel him studying the face I'm trying to hide.

I think back to the day Shelly ran out of here and Mr. Wolfe sprang this information on me. I realize now it was all part of his plan. He lied to me every time he opened his mouth, and this was just another one of those lies. I gave him the benefit of the doubt, and he took it, because that's what a thief does. He takes anything he can. He's nothing like Jackie Robinson. Jackie gives everything he can.

Dr. Richter breathes deeply and sits back in the chair. "I couldn't save him, Joey, but I certainly didn't kill him." He pauses and I take a peek. His eyes are focused on the living room wall with the big long crack. I think that's where I'll hang Mr. Friedman's painting.

"Your father had what's called angina pectoris, which, as you can guess, has to do with the heart. I prescribed medication, but I also told him to cut out the heavy meals, the heavy lifting at the store, and the cigarettes.

"Your father hid it well, but he was very anxious about giving his family a good life. He worked round the clock and you couldn't convince him to slow down. He was incredibly focused and determined."

"So you're saying he worked himself to death." He doesn't answer. I guess it wouldn't have mattered where we lived— De Bullion, Outremont, Westmount, Russia, or Timbuktu. Pa would have worked just as hard no matter what, no matter where, as long as he could give us what he never had.

"That's why you told me to have some fun."

"That's why I told you to have some fun." He smiles in a sad kind of way. "You're so very much like him."

"You sure seem to know a lot about my pa," I say.

"I knew him a long time. We first met around your age."

"Wait, what?" Now he's got a big old grin.

"He used to sit alone against a tree and watch me and my friends play ball. One day we asked him if he wanted to join in. He didn't speak a word of English and didn't know anything about the game, beyond what he'd seen us do. But I tell you, Joey, he had a good arm. And he was fast."

"My pa?" Now I'm the one in shock.

"Yeah," he chuckles. "He played once in a while but, even back then, he worked long hours to support his family. Sound familiar?"

"Yes, sir."

"At some point, he moved away to work and I didn't see him again until he and your mother walked into the Herzl with a tiny you in his arms." He smiles and stares off like he's remembering something. Then he looks right at me.

"Don't ever think for a moment he wanted to leave you."

My eyes tear up, my nose tingles, and I can feel my face redden. Dr. Richter pretends not to notice.

"There's a great quote in this book," he says as he reaches for *How to Win Friends & Influence People*. "'People rarely succeed at anything unless they have fun doing it.'"

"You kidding?" I ask suspiciously. That seems a little too perfect.

"Not kidding at all," he laughs. "This is a great gift for you. I hope ours can compare." He cocks his chin toward the pile of envelopes. "Go on, open it."

I pick up the envelope and the butter knife to slice the top open. I pull out two tickets to tomorrow night's Game 6 of the Little World Series with the Montreal Royals. With Jackie Robinson.

"Dr. Richter, I can't ..." even finish my sentence. I'm awestruck.

"It's your bar mitzvah present, Joey. Nothing more, nothing less. Oh, and don't worry, I cleared it with your mother, being *Erev* Yom Kippur and all. You get a pass to skip the most important Jewish holiday for this once-in-a-lifetime event." Dr. Richter winks at Ma, who had quietly walked up behind me. His eyes flicker with amusement. He's taking pleasure in leaving me speechless.

"Amazing," I whisper.

"While you invest all that money on your road to controlling your own destiny and becoming rich, I still insist you have fun every now and then."

"Did you give my pa the same advice?"

"Absolutely." He nods at the gift clasped in my hand and smiles that big infectious smile. He pats my leg and stands up to leave.

"Dr. Richter," I say before he steps away. "Mr. Friedman is an amazing painter. You should check out his work sometime."

"Thanks for the tip." He smiles so wide his whole face wrinkles, then he crosses the room to Shelly. Ma takes his seat.

"Mr. Wolfe thought the robbery would change everything," I say. "He's like the boy Jody, from *The Red Pony*. He dreamed those same things Jody dreams about—the high life, rubbing shoulders with sheriffs and presidents."

"Well, I haven't read the book, but from what I can tell from your book reports"—Ma stresses the "s" in reports—"I'd say you're right." She laces her fingers, places them on her lap, and leans back.

"But we can't both be Jody."

"Why not?" Her eyes sweep my face and lock with mine. My heart beats faster and my stomach feels tight.

"Because I don't want to be like Mr. Wolfe!" Am I shaking? I feel like I'm shaking. "He only cared about himself. All he wanted was ..."

Oh, no. Oh no oh no oh no. His words from the restaurant make me want to throw up. *I also want to be respectable and have lots of money and move out of this hell hole, just like you.*

Just like me.

Just like him.

"I'm not like him. Maybe I was. But I'm not anymore!"

"What do you mean?" she asks calmly, her right leg swinging slowly over her left.

"I'm going to pay Mrs. Wolfe the money I owe Mr. Wolfe with my bar mitzvah money."

"That's a wonderful thing to do. But it means you won't be able to refill your West of Park Avenue fund."

"Yeah. But it also means a clear conscience."

"You just grew up before my eyes."

I know it sounds weird, but her take-on-the-world smile looks kind of sad.

"I think the new man of the house deserves his bar mitzvah present." She slips me one more envelope.

I examine the white letter-size envelope. My name is written on the front, along with *On your bar mitzvah day*.

It's not Ma's handwriting, though.

It's Pa's.

My hands shaking, I slit open the envelope without slitting my fingers—I know, I know, it's a butter knife, but I'm really shaking this time—and look inside. I take out the letter first and read it.

Dear Joey,

One particular January day, I made an impulsive buy. I was feeling very lucky and incredibly happy. Your ma had just told me she was pregnant with you. Now that you're a man, I present this to you. I hope it's a winner.

Mazel tov on your big day. I'm so proud of you.

Love, Pa.

I pull out the second piece of paper and unfold it. It's a stock certificate. I have one share of Gold Mountain Tobacco. I have one share in Simon Bernstein's company.

"He put every cent he had into it. It's worth almost twenty times what he bought it for," Ma states proudly. "You're not the only one who reads the business pages." She winks, making me laugh. Business pages. That torn-out piece of newsprint from January 1933 that flew out of Pa's Montreal Capital and Commerce piggy bank. That was from the day he bought this.

I look back at the certificate. I own a piece of Gold Mountain. I'm Simon Bernstein's business partner! Okay, maybe not with one share, but still. Pa did just like Simon Bernstein said to do. He knew what to do all along. He saved his money and invested it in the grocery store, in something worthwhile, and then found bigger and better opportunities. But he didn't do it for himself. He did it for his family.

I want Pa. I did everything with him. I can't do it all without him. I've been trying to fool everyone into thinking I could—run the store, start lots of businesses, make loads of money, take care of Ma and David—but I'm pretty sure the only person I've been fooling is me. I wonder if Pa's disappointed in me. Maybe I should ask David.

I look around to find David still with Shelly reading him the baseball news. She came. She came here to celebrate with me. I know it's not like she skipped out on her own party, but still ... she's here. I get up off the dilapidated chair—which really is incredibly cozy—and amble over to Shelly and David.

"Hi," I say.

"Hi," she replies. Out of the corner of my eye, I can see David looking back and forth between us, like he's watching Jackie Robinson caught between second and third. He rolls his eyes and wanders away, but not before bumping into my back and forcing me to take a step closer to Shelly. What a little ... fixer.

"Thank you for coming," I start.

"It took a bit of convincing." She bites one side of her bottom lip.

"I bet. I was a complete idiot."

"I don't disagree."

"I really am sorry."

HEATHER CAMLOT

"Me, too." We stand there smiling at each other, me swaying on my feet, Shelly moving her left hand up and down along her right arm.

Thwack. Something strikes me in the back, forcing me to step in so close to Shelly, the smell of lavender goes right up my nose and somehow makes me lean in even more and kiss her on the cheek. It was only two seconds, but I swear my heart was pounding as fast as when Shelly's dog chased me and Ben through the park. Applause and laughter bring me back to Shelly, back to the living room, back to Ma and Dr. Richter watching on, a little too amused. I look around, completely hot in the face, and see a tattered baseball lying by my feet. David. He really does have a good arm. He could be the next Jackie Robinson.

Chapter 30

APPEAL PLAY

66 *He came into my office more than once, and he'd say,*
'Nobody knows what I'm going through.'
But he never mentioned quitting. 99
– Mel Jones, Montreal Royals general manager

As soon as Shelly and Dr. Richter leave the flat, I race over to Ben's—the second time I've ever been to his house in my entire life.

Mrs. Wolfe opens the door with the most welcoming face I've ever seen. Not exactly what I was expecting from a woman whose husband was killed twenty-four hours ago and whose son just came back from the hospital. She doesn't look scared or sound nervous like when I came by yesterday. She just looks kind of tired.

"I'm sorry about ... what happened."

"Everything happens for a reason," she says, then hugs me tight.

I don't think I believe that but I don't say anything. Mrs.

Wolfe points me to Ben's bedroom. I follow the light blue hallway, ceiling lamps casting a yellow light and dark shadows on the photos hanging along the wall. Photos of Ben and his ma. Photos with me, even with David. Some with a smiling Mr. Wolfe and Ben, when he was little. They were a happy family, once upon a time. I wonder what happened.

I open the door at the end of the hall to find Ben lying in bed with a stack of *Movie Life* magazines by his side and his face hidden by last month's issue with some actor on the cover. His walls are plastered with movie posters.

"Hi," I say, sticking by the doorway.

"Hi," he replies, putting down the magazine. His skin is gray and his eyes dull.

"How're you doing?"

"I dunno. I'm all right, I guess," he says, sitting himself up against two pillows and waving me over. "I have to go talk to some social worker every week until they think I'm better. They think I'm crazy because I'm glad he's dead. They think there's something wrong with that. But they don't know him, you know?"

I just nod my head and swallow hard.

"If that other guy at the bank missed and only hurt him, I'd have got the beating of a lifetime and I'd probably be the dead one."

Ben has never uttered the word "beating" to me before, never admitted what'd been going on at home. I only got to see what he couldn't hide—a limp, two black eyes. All covered up with fantastic lies. I never believed them, but I always let him think I did.

"Bet the Morality Squad is having a good laugh. First that gangster guy Harry Davis this summer, now my pa. Everyone on their vice hit list is getting killed off, one by one, without them lifting a finger." I'm pretty sure that's not exactly how the police were hoping to clean up the city, but I keep it to myself.

"Why didn't you ever tell me how bad it was?" My throat burns. I try to clear it but it just feels raw, like salt water on a wound.

"It would've been different. You would've been different. I was a normal kid in a normal family at your place. Working at a grocery store, playing with my brothers, eating dinner with my parents. I miss your pa, Joey."

"Yeah, me, too." We're quiet. Not uncomfortable quiet, just the kind where you have to take a minute to digest everything. But this is all way more than a minute can handle.

"You know, I hated whenever someone called Pa a real kind man, a real *mensch*. I figured it meant we'd always be poor and stuck on De Bullion forever. It's like Leo Durocher said a couple of months ago, 'Nice guys wind up in last place.'

Something like that, anyway."

"Who's Leo Durocher?"

"Manager of the Dodgers. Point is, Pa was the nicest man in the world; he'd give you the shirt off his back, and because of that, he had nothing. And I always thought, I never want to be like that; I never want to be like him."

"I can understand that," Ben says. I'm sure he's thinking about his own pa.

"Everything used to be so black and white, you know, good, bad, happy, sad, love, hate. I hated my pa, but not really. I was just angry at him. Rabbi Gottlieb told me a *mensch* is someone who's honest and trustworthy. After everything this summer, I just think: I hope someday I'll be like him."

"The bar mitzvah worked! That was man-speak if I ever heard it. Well done, my boy! Well done!" Ben says the last bit in his wealthy British landowner voice, then sits right up and shakes my hand, over and over again, making me crack up.

"Man-speak? So I'm sounding all adult-like now because of one hour in synagogue?"

"Guess so. That was the most grownup thing I've ever heard you say."

"Great. Swell."

Ben lies back against his pillows, a smile stretched across his face.

"Joey?"

"Yeah?"

"You are like your pa. You are a real kind man, a real *mensch*."

Hearing Ben say those words to me makes me want to laugh and cry at the same time. Nothing is black and white anymore. Instead, I say, "So I've been told," remembering my conversation with Dr. Richter earlier today. I look at Ben, staring up at the posters on his ceiling. "What's going to happen now, with you?"

"We're going to live happily ever after. Just like in the movies." There's no sarcasm in his voice and he smiles just a little. Then he bolts up and his smile widens into a big old grin. "I can't believe you saw your first movie today!"

"Adele let me in," I say with a laugh.

"Without me! How could you?"

"What's the deal with you two, anyway? I never knew you two 'associated' with each other," I say, using Mr. Wolfe's word. He knew all about Ben and Adele. I never did.

"Associated?"

"Never mind. So?"

"We've been doing stuff together for a while. We didn't tell anyone we were friends 'cause I didn't want my pa to find out. I guess I was trying to protect her, like your pa was protecting you and David. When he got Mr. Abelson that bank job, that's when I realized he knew all along. Anything he weaseled his way into turned real bad. I'm glad you're okay."

How many times has Ben protected me without me knowing? I could have been shot, killed, taken away from Ma, from David, from school, from home.

"You knew what your pa was up to all along, didn't you?"

He nods slowly. "I tried to tell you. You wouldn't listen to me."

"Yeah." I concentrate on rolling and unrolling one of the magazines from Ben's bed. "Thank you."

"For what?"

"For ... for being my friend."

"You were the only one I could get!" We crack up again, and I think back to how much I've learned about Ben and me and Pa these past few of months.

"Oh, wait, I have something you can really be thankful for." He rolls out of bed and signals for me to get off. "Give me a hand."

We flip the heavy mattress, blankets flying all over the floor, and let it drop back onto the frame. He climbs on top, yanks off a piece of masking tape, and sticks his hand into a slit right in the middle, pulling out two bundles of money tied up in rubber bands.

"Okay, flip." The mattress crashes down. He climbs back on.

"Where'd you get all that?" I ask.

He hands me one bundle. I don't take it. "It's yours. It's the money my old man stole from you."

"What?"

"The money he stole from the store"—he lifts the bundle—"and from everyone else"—he taps the other—"when he was 'testing his strategies.' I had to tell him where the safe was, Joey. He beat it out of me. I'm real sorry."

I think about the morning after the robbery and Ben limping as we walked to get David. I knew he didn't trip playing basketball like he told me. I also think about all those times Mr. Wolfe was following me. Probably checking to make sure I didn't go to the bank.

"How'd you get the money?" I ask suspiciously.

"I stole it back from him, Joey." He grins. "He did teach me one useful skill."

"What, safe-cracking?" I say with a laugh.

"Yeah," he says real low, looking away.

"Keep it—I owe your pa money for the hospital bill."

"You're the insane one, not me, you know that? Fine, Mr. No Credit, count out what you *think* you owe and take the rest."

"That sounds fair."

"You should take it all, but I'm tired of fighting."

I pick up the bundle with the slip of paper that has my

name on it, count out the money, give him his share, and pocket the rest of what was stolen from the store.

"You're going to need this. Now." I don't fill in the rest.

"I guess. Maybe. But I'm not worried, Joey. I'm really not. The money's yours."

"But I also owe you back pay for all your time at the store. Never really crossed my mind you were working, just kinda loitering," I say, trying to make him smile.

"I would've paid every cent I got to stay there twenty-four hours a day." That shuts us up good for a bit. Ben keeps staring at the ceiling. I stare at him.

"Well, if you change your mind, I could use some help at the store and I'd pay you for real."

"Okay. I'll think about it."

"You should bring that other money to the police."

"Yeah, that's the plan."

I pick up the blankets from the floor, then head to the door.

"Everything work out with you and your girlfriend?"

"Yeah," I say, not arguing this time about whether Shelly's my girlfriend or not. I think she is. I hope she is. Guess I should ask her, just to be sure.

"Will you come back tomorrow?" He pulls the blankets over him.

"You mean you're not coming to work?"

He laughs. "Ma wants me home for a bit."

"Then I guess I'll have to come here."

"Can you bring me a box of Cracker Jack?"

"I'll bring you two."

"Whoa, don't get carried away with all that money in your pocket!"

"I'll even go see Old Mr. Friedman and get you the October issue of *Movie Life*."

"I don't know who you are anymore, big spender!"

"Bye, Ben."

"Bye, Joey."

As I close the bedroom door, I peek in one last time. Ben's eyes are closed. But he flashes his Hollywood smile. I love that smile.

Chapter 31

CURTAIN CALL

66 *He has proven his worth in the minors and is definitely ready for the big leagues.* **99**
– Sportswriter Wendell Smith

"Are we there yet?" David asks in that real whiny-kid kind of way.

"Just a bit further." I can feel him studying my face for a clue as to where we're going, but I keep my eyes looking out the streetcar window. This is the furthest east we've ever been. Yes, east. It's like a whole new world. A whole new amazing world. The sun is already down, but I can still see leaves drifting to the ground, and I consider my plan for the raking business. I don't think it would be much fun and, like Dale Carnegie said and Dr. Richter pointed out, it's hard to be successful at something if it isn't any fun. I'll just watch the leaves fall for a while and reconsider the plan next year. Yeah, next year. I've started thinking long-term.

"All right, give me your hand and close your eyes."

"Aw, come on, Joey."

"Ma said you have to do what I say," I remind him, but with one of his signature I-know-something-you-don't-know smirks. I knew the moment I saw the baseball tickets that I'd have to keep it secret from David or else he'd drive me and Ma nuts until game time.

"Fine," he says, rolling his eyes before shutting them. We get off the streetcar with every single other passenger. Instead of losing him in a part of town I know nothing about, I lift him up in my arms until we're near, then lower him to the ground and turn him to face the right way.

"All right, open." David does as he's told. He rubs his eyes, blinks really hard, and rubs them again. Then his mouth drops open. Although we're being jostled by people trying to get to the entrance of Delorimier Stadium, David doesn't move.

"Whoa … do you think we can hear it all from out here? Maybe if we get a little closer?"

"Probably, but I think it's better to go inside, no?"

"In … inside? We're going inside?"

"If you can unglue yourself from the pavement."

"I don't know if I can, Joey. I really don't." I laugh at the look of awe—or maybe it's just plain fear—on David's face. So worth not telling him. I lift him up again and make our way to the entrance.

"*Avez-vous des billets*? Do you 'ave tickets?" asks the man at the gate. I pull out the two tickets, David studying them like he's trying to make sure they're real.

"Box seats, dat way," he tilts his head in the direction we're supposed to follow, but now both David and I are frozen with our mouths open.

"Box seats?" we say at the same time. I never looked at the tickets that closely.

The man grins. "Nearly dee best der are. You know a player?"

I shake my head. "Bar mitzvah present."

"*Ben*, it's one 'eck of a present." He ushers us in and continues his ticket-taking for the throngs of people behind us.

"I'm gonna have a lot to tell my friends at school on Monday, Joey," David says real low. I think it's safe to say we're both blown away by how huge this all is.

We make our way to our seats, between home plate and first base, so close to the playing field we could actually spit and hit a player—not that we would, but that's how close. Past the outfield, a big Gold Mountain Tobacco sign sits on top of a building for all of us at the ballpark to see. Mr. Bernstein sure knows how to promote his product, just like business basic #10 says to do. I wonder if that's his factory underneath. I wonder if Mr. Bernstein is watching the ball game from there. I know I would.

We stare out at the empty field, David in total awe. Even though the weather's warmed up, Ma insisted he wear the royal blue set Mrs. Abelson knitted for him. I pop off the toque and hand him his baseball hat. It suits him. He looks happy and relaxed, like this is where he's meant to be. Maybe it is. Maybe one day I'll be sitting in the stands like I am now, watching my little brother play ball. The next Jackie Robinson.

A crash of cheers startles me and I look onto the field to see one, then two, then all the players from the Montreal Royals and the Louisville Colonels coming out of the dugouts. There's got to be 20,000 spectators in the stands. All here to see what could be the last game of the series, standing at 3–2 for the Royals. All here to witness what could be our chance to finally win a Little World Series. All here to cheer on the greatness that is Jackie Robinson.

The first inning flies by like a dream. I'm still trying to process the fact that we're actually here, that this is actually happening right before our very eyes. I can't help but giggle, and David joins in.

As the game rounds into the second inning, the score is still 0–0. I look around our seats—everyone is so well-dressed, you'd think we were in *shul*, men in their three-piece suits and fedoras, women in their best jackets and skirts, furs and trench coats draped over their laps.

"Buy me some peanuts and Cracker Jack ..." David hums.

"Are you singing or asking?" I grin. I get the grin now. It kind of makes you feel powerful.

"Eh?" He stops singing and looks at me confused. "I ... can we? But I'm sure it costs lots of money, and you need to save for a house on the west side and all ..." I wave over the concessions guy, carrying a full tray of snacks.

"Peanuts and Cracker Jack, please." I turn to David who is wide-eyed and salivating. "Life's about more than just money, David. You gotta have some fun," I say. I've been thinking a lot about what Dr. Richter and Ma have been trying to tell me, about having fun and going to university. Jackie Robinson went to college and university and look at him now. It's not so common for kids in my neighborhood to go to school for so long, but I think that's what Pa would want me to be saving for. Mine and David's future. It's not so bad living on De Bullion. For now. We have friends real close by, a good enough business to bring money in, and a flat so spotless, no cockroach would dare come in. I'll let the Gold Mountain stock get even bigger for a bit. Then, when the time's right, we'll buy a real nice house on the west side of Park Avenue.

"You sure you're okay?" David asks, his face all crinkled up like he's staring directly into the sun. Or a floodlight.

"Yeah, David. I'm fine." I hand over some of my bar mitzvah money for the food. David quickly removes his mittens and digs in.

"You want some?" he asks, running the peanuts through his fingers.

"No, thanks."

David nods and munches on his peanuts. He laces his fingers in mine. I hold on to them tight.

"You're a good kid, David. Don't ever grow up."

"I don't plan to." He looks up at me with those smiling eyes and that loopy grin.

Crack! Royal Dixie "Homer" Howell doubles down to left field, and our Lew Riggs, who had walked to first base, runs to second ... to third ... to home plate. He slides around the Colonels catcher and scores the first run of the game! David and I jump out of our seats, like everyone else in the stadium, and hoot like mad. Now Al Campanis steps up to the plate ... steadies his bat ... slices one down the right ... and sends Homer home for another run. It's 2–0! The crowd is so wild, we can't hear a thing the announcer is saying, but who cares? It's 2–0!

"We're winning, Joey. We're going to win, I just know it!"

David's left leg is bouncing up and down. I put my hand on it to make it stop, but there's no use. That leg is really excited.

So far, the game really belongs to Al Campanis and Dixie Howell, batting in players, but Jackie Robinson's been doing some great fielding. Especially in the fourth.

"Don't worry about that smash, Joey! That Colonel's not going to make it, even with Les Burge's fumble. Look! Jackie's on it!" If his baseball playing career doesn't work out, David could definitely be the next Royals play-by-play man. "See how easy he just tossed that ball? Out!"

Jackie Robinson comes through again in the sixth, with a blink-and-you-missed-it double play with shortstop Al Campanis and first baseman Les Burge. Yes! So much for "playing" ball. This is full-on combat. David's concentrating too hard to speak anymore. Doesn't matter much, with both those legs going his words would come out all rattled, anyway, like pulling the wagon over cobblestone.

Jackie Robinson's up to bat again in the eighth and you can see how much Colonels pitcher Harry Dorish wants him gone. It's not going to happen! Jackie hits a single. But Dorish can't leave it alone. He's making all these fake throws to get Jackie out on first, and the fans are screaming at him. When he finally goes back to pitching, he walks our Tom Tatum, moving Jackie to second and then—can you believe this guy?—he fake throws all over again. What an amateur!

The atmosphere in the stadium is electric and it makes me feel a little light-headed, giddy. I look around at the thousands of people in the stands. In regular life, we'd probably have nothing to say to each other, probably never even run into each other. But here ... well, everyone's here for the same reason. I wonder if we all have the same butterfly feeling in our bellies, too, like a group queasiness.

The score is still 2–0 for the Royals in the ninth. The inning isn't looking too good. But then comes another double play, between Jackie Robinson and Les Burge.

"They're outta there!" David says, jumping out of his seat again. "That's two gone, Joey. We just need one more. One more!" And Royals third baseman Lew Riggs delivers, stopping Colonel Otto Denning in his tracks.

Game over!

Do you know what rapture sounds like? It sounds like twenty thousand baseball fans roaring with pride. It sounds like David's silence, watching Jackie Robinson play ball. It sounds like Mr. Friedman's sigh of relief, enough air to fill twenty million balloons, finding out the Nazis will be punished. It sounds like Ma telling me Ben is all right. It sounds like Shelly forgiving me for being a jerk. It sounds like the Montreal Royals making history.

HEATHER CAMLOT

We won.

"Jackie was the only one to get two hits, did you see, Joey?" David says, tears in his eyes. "It's 'cause he crowds the plate and he holds his bat high and he doesn't let the other guys know what he's thinking. Did you see, Joey? Did you?"

Fans all around the stadium run onto the field, police and ushers unable to keep them back, everyone screaming, "WE WANT ROBINSON. WE WANT ROBINSON." David and I stay where we are, not wanting to get crushed in the mob scene. As soon as manager Clay Hopper comes out of the dugout, people lift him up on their shoulders and parade him around the diamond. Curt Davis comes out next and gets the same treatment.

"Will Jackie go on the field, too, Joey?" David's eyes dart everywhere, trying to find his idol.

"I have no idea, David."

"There he is, Joey! There he is! Can we go on the field?" David points in the same direction from where Clay Hopper and Curt Davis entered and there's Jackie, in his everyday clothes. The fans immediately hoist him into the air and parade him around. David and I run down a few steps to get even closer to the field, but there's no way we can get anywhere near Jackie Robinson. Everyone on the field is trying to touch him and hug him and kiss him and get a souvenir by tearing at his clothes.

David and I cheer ourselves hoarse. When Jackie finally leaves the field, David and I start making our way out of the stadium. Without any clue where we're going, we run into another crowd.

"What's going on?" I ask a fellow who has his fedora pressed against his pinstriped suit and is standing on tiptoe to look at what amounts to a closed door.

"We're waiting for Jackie to come out," he answers without turning his head.

I look down at David. "Should we?"

His little face, already drained by the ballgame, lights up. I lift him onto my shoulders so he can see better.

"R-r-o-y-e ... Royals ... l-o-lo-k-e ... l-o-k-e-r ... loker ... oh, locker, Royals locker r-o ... r-o-m ... room. It says 'Royals locker room' on the door, Joey!"

"How'd you read that?" I ask, shocked.

"Mr. Friedman's a real good reader. He reads all day at the newspaper stand! Says he's gonna teach me to paint next."

"Amazing!"

From his perch, David reports that the door keeps trying to open but the people are blocking the way. Finally, it opens wide, and Jackie Robinson has no choice but to jump into the packed crowd and work his way through.

"There he is, Joey! I can see him. Mr. Robinson! Mr.

Robinson!" he cries as loud as his high-pitched voice can. I look up just in time to see his eyes widen in mad joy and a beam stretch across his entire face. "He's smiling at me, Joey! He's smiling at me!"

And you know what? Jackie Robinson really was smiling at David. It's right here in the black and white photo on the sports page, carefully cut out of the newspaper and stuck on the wall in David's hiding spot behind the grocery store counter.

I'm going to buy us season's tickets one day. I will. You watch.

Language Glossary

YIDDISH

A mise meshune oyf dir: a horrible death to you

A sheynem dank: thank you very much

Bar mitzvah: coming of age ceremony for boys age 13. Bat mitzvah is for girls age 12, and b'nai mitzvah is a plural form.

Bima: raised platform or stage in a synagogue

Bist krank?: are you sick?

Boychik: term of endearment for a young boy or man

Chutzpah: nerve, guts

Erev: literally, evening. Erev Yom Kippur refers to the day before or eve of Yom Kippur.

Gut: good

Hilf: help

Karnatzel: long and thin cured beef sausage stick; a Montreal Jewish delicacy

L'chaim: a toast, to life

Lox: smoked salmon

Mazel tov: good luck, congratulations

Mensch: a decent, honorable person

Neyn: no

Nu: so? well?

Oy/oy vey: expression of dismay, like "oh" or "oh, boy"; shorter form of "Oh, woe is me!"

Rugelach: a flaky filled cookie shaped like a crescent

Schlep: drag

Shalom: hello

Shlump: slob

Shmegegge: untalented, unintelligent, immoral person; idler, fool

Shul: synagogue

Torah: the first part of the Jewish bible, consisting of the five books of Moses, and the most important Jewish text

Vos machstu: how are you?

Yarmulke: a skullcap, a kippah

FRENCH

Avez-vous des billets?: do you have tickets?

Ben: French oral expression for "okay, well…"

Château: castle

Et fils: and sons

Glossary of Baseball Terminology

At bat: a hitter's appearance at home plate

Appeal play: when a defensive team player tells the umpire about an unseen infraction

Bases empty: no runners on the field, the only scoring opportunity being with the hitter at bat

Brushback: a pitch with the intention to intimidate

Called up: promoted from the minor leagues

Charging the mound: when a batter runs up to the pitcher to get retribution after being hit by a ball

Circus catch: a spectacular, very acrobatic, catch

Crosstown rivalry: when two teams are located in the same city

Curtain call: a player's return to the field to take a bow after an outstanding play

Expanded roster: when the number of players on a team increases under special circumstances

Force play: when a runner has no choice but to move to the next base so the batter can go to first

Freeze the hitter: a pitch so unexpected that the batter doesn't have a chance to react

Governor's Cup: the trophy awarded to the International League champion, a farm club/minor AAA team in Major League Baseball. The Montreal Royals won it seven times.

Grand slam: a home run with bases loaded

HEATHER CAMLOT

Ground rules: special rules for a particular baseball field

Hit the deck: batter gets out of a pitch coming right at him by dropping to the ground

Hot stove league: talking baseball during the winter

Intentional walk: batter gets a free ride to first base, on purpose

Interleague play: games played by teams outside their regular major league, like one team from the National League and the other from the American League

Jelly legs: when a hitter is tricked out of proper batting stance

Little World Series: the championship playoff between the leading minor league teams in the International League and the American Association. The Montreal Royals won this three times.

Lock him up: signing a player long-term

Losing streak: loss after loss

Money pitch: the golden throw reserved for a critical moment in a game

One-game wonder: a player who only gets to play one major league game, and does well, before being sent back to the minors or benched

Patient hitter: a batter who waits for a pitch he thinks he can hit

Pinch hitter: a substitute batter brought in when the lineup's current hitter isn't up to the job

Pink hat: an opportunistic rather than loyal fan

Productive out: when a batter strikes out but runners still move forward

Sacrifice hit: a batter intentionally bunts and gets out so a runner can advance

Screaming line drive: a hard, low hit that moves fast enough to hit the pitcher or strong enough to knock off a fielder's glove

Stayed alive: when a batter with two strikes fouls and gets another try at bat; also, when a team finally wins in the face of elimination and will live to see another game

Visiting team: the team that goes to play at another team's stadium

Works Cited

Quotes courtesy of the *Afro-American Newspapers* (Sam Lacy); *Pittsburgh Courier* archives (Wendell Smith); Postmedia Network Inc. for the *Montreal Gazette* (Dink Carroll, Bill Reddy, Branch Rickey, Mel Jones) and *Montreal Daily Star* (Baz O'Meara, Lloyd McGowan, Clay Hopper, Frank Shaughnessy, Jean-Pierre Roy); Simon & Schuster (Dale Carnegie's *How to Win Friends & Influence People*); and *Sporting News* ("'Nice Guys' Wind Up in Last Place" headline). All rights reserved. Reprinted with permission..

Acknowledgments

My thanks first and foremost to the three Camlot siblings: my dad, Morris, for a magical tour of his old neighborhood and the stories he'd never before shared. To my uncle, Irving, for his few words and the twinkle in his eye. And to my aunt, Louise Troyansky, for the detailed answers to my relentless questions.

Thank you to Michael Redhill for the pep talk I needed to write fiction, and to Anne Laurel Carter for her mentoring, editing, and endless cheerleading.

A huge thanks to my young and adult readers for their valuable time and comments: Evan Cyr-David, Alexandre Reppin, Thomas Sorensen, Shari Becker, Loretta Garbutt, Jacqueline Guest, Marsha Moshinsky, Randal Schnoor, and Sharlene Wiseman.

Special thanks to Jason Camlot, Sylvia Camlot, Jennifer Cyr, Karen Krossing, Gerry Nott, Kevin Sylvester, and Judie Troyansky. So many varied reasons, but you each know why.

To my editor, Peter Carver, for his patience and wonderful editorial eye. I'm also grateful to Richard Dionne and Winston Stilwell at Red Deer Press.

Finally, thank you to my mom, Linda Camlot, my husband, Marc Reppin, and my children, Alex and Juliana. We made it.

HEATHER CAMLOT

Interview with
HEATHER CAMLOT

You are a Montrealer, born and bred. What led you to want to tell this particular story about a Montreal that existed long before you were born?

The Plateau is considered the hip, cool neighborhood in Montreal today. But back when my dad and his siblings grew up there, in the 1940s, it was anything but. People were poor, they were immigrants, the older generation spoke mostly Yiddish. At the same time, Montreal was one of, if not the most glamorous, most progressive, and liveliest cities in Canada. I used to ask my dad about his childhood, my uncle too, but they rarely talked about it, and even then would only mention the littlest things. So, as tends to happen, my imagination began to run free and out came *Clutch*.

What was it about Jackie Robinson's year of playing for the Montreal Royals that made you want to include his story?

It started with the fact that he was in Montreal. I had no idea that this major moment in history—never mind baseball history—began right in my own city. I had seen the statue of him in front of Olympic Stadium, but I had never thought much about it. And then I wondered how many other people didn't really know. The more I researched, the more fascinated I became. The pressure on him to succeed was tremendous.

Fortunately, Jackie Robinson's time in Montreal coincided with when I wanted to set my novel, so 1946 became the year.

One thing I think a lot of people don't know is that while he was the first to sign and all eyes were on him, Jackie Robinson was not the only black player in the 1946 minor leagues. There was Johnny Wright and later Roy Partlow, both with the Royals but demoted just months after they were hired. In the United States, Roy Campanella and Don Newcombe played with the Nashua Dodgers. They would join Robinson and the Brooklyn Dodgers in 1948 and 1949, respectively.

You have included quotes at the beginning of each chapter that have to do with the early career of Jackie Robinson. Why did you feel the quotes were important in telling Joey's story?
I wanted to share Jackie Robinson's story without him being the story and I thought quotes would be a cool, different way to do that. They are not there to say Joey's struggles are equal to Jackie Robinson's struggles—of course they're not. But they do act as guideposts. What I mean by that is we tend to follow stories about our heroes and apply them to our own lives in a way that comforts, motivates, inspires—at the very least makes us feel like we're not alone. This comes across most clearly when Dr. Richter uses Jackie Robinson as an example to talk to Joey about pressure. Joey is going through so much, he feels the world is closing in on him, and there's this great man just a short distance away that he's constantly reading about, that he can look up to and say: If he can push through, maybe I can, too.

Joey says he wants to be the man in the family, after his father's death, taking charge of the family business and seeing that they have sufficient funds to move to a home "west of Park Avenue." Why does he need to be in charge, even though he's only twelve years old?

Joey believes his father died because of where they live, their "dump of a neighborhood." He loves his family very much and would be devastated if anything happened to his mother or brother. So for him, the way to protect them is to get them out of there, but to do that he needs money. He's also constantly reading the newspaper so he knows what's going on beyond his little corner of the world and he longs to be a part of it. Finally, in Judaism, age 13 is associated with maturity, with internal change. But Joey takes it to mean full-fledged adulthood and needing to support his family and earn a living.

Joey's family name—Grosser—might be taken as a pun on the family business, a grocery store. Was that your intention?

No, it was a happy coincidence. Most of the names in the novel have special meaning. Grosser was my paternal grandmother's maiden name. I used my maternal grandmother and great-grandmother's maiden names for the character of Simon Bernstein—also coincidentally, the same initials as one of the men he was based on. Shelly's last name, Richter, is my best friend's last name and I loved the fact that it had "rich" in it. "Gold Mountain" Brewery came from my maternal grandfather's last name, Goldenberg—"berg" meaning "mountain," perfect for a story set in Montreal. Even the lettering on the store window, *Bernier et fils*, is an inside joke—I speak about baseball and hockey in the novel, but I'm a soccer fan, so the store is named after a Montreal Impact player!

Why did you decide to include Old Mr. Friedman's Holocaust story in the book?

While researching the Little League World Series in the *Montreal Daily Star*, I came across the October 1, 1946, headline: *Goering, Ribbentrop, 10 Other Top Nazis To Be Hanged*. Here was one of, if not the most important verdicts in history. *Clutch* is a story about Jewish kids in a Jewish neighborhood filled with Jewish immigrants from Europe and Russia, and set right after the war. Someone in my story had to have some sort of connection to the Holocaust. Mr. Friedman became that person. Through him, I could also share lesser-known events like the degenerate art exhibition and the voyage of the St. Louis. History's lessons are invaluable.

Can you say something about the challenge of locating a story in a real historical setting? What sort of research does that involve?

It's definitely challenging, because you want to be as accurate as possible. I pored through newspapers, read books and websites, contacted various organizations and experts for details big and small. My dad took me on a tour of the Plateau when I started writing. I drove around myself and took lots of pictures. I consulted all kinds of maps. I bombarded my mom and aunts with a thousand questions. My parents' friends shared childhood stories. For the ballgame, I read at least half a dozen news stories from Canada and the United States, compared and contrasted, and teased out my own play by play. I quadruple-checked everything and I hope I got it all right. I did take some artistic license. For example, I doubt that there was a newsstand in Fletcher's Field or that *The Red Pony* was being taught in school yet, the Bernstein mansion is a mashup of a few different Westmount homes, and I referenced a *Sporting News* article that wasn't yet published.

What was the intention in your choice of the book's title— Clutch?

The word clutch has a few meanings, all of which relate to the story. It means an evil power or control one person holds over another, like Mr. Wolfe has on Joey. It means to tightly grab or hold onto someone or something, like Joey does after stopping David from crossing St. Lawrence Blvd. It also means to be successful in a high-pressure situation with a lot at stake, like Jackie Robinson's clutch performance when he stepped onto the field at Jersey City's Roosevelt Stadium on April 18, 1946, for his first game with the Royals.

This is your first published novel. What have you learned in the process of writing it, and what advice would you give to young people wanting to tell their own stories?

Writing a novel is *a lot* of work. When you think it's done, it's not. I've written at least twenty versions. I learned about the issues of using real quotes, real people, real places, real products—you have to be very careful about how you include them and you may need permission. Let others read the manuscript and listen to what they say; they see and hear the things that aren't working. Research, research, research—it enriches a story in so many ways. Finally, keep going. I wasn't sure *Clutch* would ever be published. But here it is.

Thank you, Heather.